I0619509

KISSED CYBORG

BOUND BY HER - BOOK 3

NELLIE C. LIND

Sense of Romance

High-level romance for romance lovers!

Kissed Cyborg
Bound by Her - Book 3
Copyright © Nellie C. Lind 2019
Cover and layout: Nellie C. Lind
Editor: Chrissy Szarek
Publisher: Sense of Romance
ISBN: 978-91-983128-2-9

PREFACE

Fifty years ago, the scientific and medical company, MedAct created the first male cyborgs. Their creator was the founder of MedAct, Carolyn Williams, and it gave every woman out there the opportunity to create the *perfect* man.

From the moment the cyborgs opened their eyes and became aware of the world, they were in love with the woman that'd designed them.

Society was told cyborgs couldn't exist without the bond to a human woman, and the cyborgs who survived the death of their bound one went crazy, even became dangerous. The only way to help them was to find a new bound one.

It was all a lie.

Celise Campbell, a MedAct doctor, learned it the hard way when her cyborg Wind almost died when his bond was being transferred to her from his previous bound one. The bond turned out to be nothing more but a poison programmed to be released into the cyborg's system the moment their bound one died.

Sometimes, the poison failed to kill the cyborgs, and those who survived were the ones who knew the truth.

They became the Fighters, led by the first cyborg ever created; Nightmare.

Their goal; destroy the bond and set the cyborgs free.

The answer seems to lie in the secret female cyborg program.

CHAPTER 1

"Release me." Silver glared at Nightmare and pulled the chains that held him to the wall in the windowless room. It consisted of a bed, and a bathroom hidden behind a curtain.

"You know I can't do that." The leader crossed his arms over his chest. "You need to be restrained once I bring Faye here. I can't risk you hurting her."

Anger boiled in his veins. "I'll kill her if she touches me."

The big cyborg's glare darkened. "No, you won't. You need her. You're dead without her. I don't know how much longer your body can go on without the two remaining flashes. The light in your eyes is so bright it's blinding, and it's not going to go away."

"You're signing me up for a certain death."

"No, I'm prolonging your death." Nightmare moved closer. "What good will it do if you die now? If you bind yourself to her, we'll get time to find the answer to how to remove the bond. Besides, I need you. I've already lost Hunter. I can't lose you, too."

Silver glared at the Fighters' leader. "So, you expect me to move to Glaswell once I'm bound to her and live a sweet fairytale life?"

He shrugged. "Why not? We could use an inside-man. Imagine the possibilities. We have one of MedAct's doctors on our side now. Celise has seen the truth and believes us. Imagine what we can accomplish if we get one foot inside MedAct as well? Entering Glaswell is one step in that direction."

"Why didn't you ask this of the other Fighters who bound themselves again?" He snorted.

"Because I didn't trust them. All of them, including Hunter, had to delete all their information about us because they ended up in MedAct's hands. *You* won't have to. You'll go directly to Glaswell with Faye. Celise will be your supervisor, and Jade will believe anything she says. And once you're there, you'll be able to talk to Hunter, see if you can activate his memory, and bring him back."

Everything inside Silver protested against the idea, but at the same time, he needed Faye to finish the bonding. "You can't ask this of me."

Nightmare raised an eyebrow. "Do you want to die?"

"No."

"Then you'll find a way to make this happen. Right now, *you* are our only card in, our only chance. It's a chance of a lifetime. It'll never come again if we allow it to pass us by."

"You're asking the impossible of me. Do you really want me to go through the same thing you did with Carolyn?"

The leader's expression tensed. "It's only for a short time. With Celise's help, we'll be able to find the answer sooner than later."

Silver sighed. "Don't make me do this."

Nightmare headed for the door. "I'll bring Faye here in a few minutes. I'll make sure you both have everything you need while you're in here, but what happens is completely up to you. But remember, Silver. Our fate lies in your hands now." He left the room.

CHAPTER 2

"Oh, wow," Faye said as she watched the Fighter.

His name was Sense. He had the most amazing eyes she'd ever seen, and he held a card game in his hands.

Somehow, he'd managed to make the card she'd chosen to disappear, and she couldn't figure out how.

"That was really impressive. Where did you learn to do that?"

He gave her a wide smile. "My late bound one's brother was a magician. He could perform all kinds of tricks, and he taught me a few."

Since Celise had healed him, he'd been all over the place and full of energy. His pain was gone, but from time to time, Sense paused in his tracks and shook his head as he pressed his hand against his chest.

Faye could only assume his damaged bond was messing with him, but she restrained herself from asking. It was probably the last thing he wanted to talk about right now.

Phoenix, who sat next to her on the couch, laughed. "Don't be shy, Sense. You can do a lot more than that." He glanced at Faye. "He and his late bound one performed a few times with her brother. I saw one of their shows, and it sure was quite something."

Pride shone in Sense's eyes, but there was also a hint of sadness. "Those were wonderful times."

Faye looked around the big gathering room. It was filled with everything from computers to pool tables. She was far below underground, inside Nightmare's headquarters, surrounded by Fighters.

Other than Sense and Phoenix, there were seven other Fighters, all enjoying themselves, but the quick and sneaky looks they gave her made her swallow hard.

There was no escape if one of them snapped, but she'd chanced it instead of staying in her room alone and slowly getting bored out of her mind. Besides, she'd gotten quite fond of some of the Fighters.

Phoenix was one of them.

He was one-of-a-kind, with his androgynist appearance. He didn't have the physic of a bodybuilder like most Fighters. Instead, he reminded her of an elf from all the fairy tales she'd read as a child. Even the way he moved had a feminine touch, and it made him appear beautiful and appealing. His long, copper-red hair was a finishing touch to the masterpiece he was.

Faye was curious about his bound one, and what'd

9

happened to her.

Most Fighters seemed to have taken a liking to her, but Phoenix even more so. He barely left her side.

She turned her gaze back to Sense. "Do you wish you could go back?"

His smile faded. "No. Not with the knowledge I have today. I do miss my bound one. She was an amazing person, but I don't ever want to be bound again. My pain isn't as great as it was, thanks to Celise. The ache in my heart I can live with until we find an answer to the bond. It shouldn't be long. If we're lucky, maybe a year or two."

"How about you?" she asked Phoenix.

He tilted his head, as if in thought. "Honestly, I'd love nothing more but to have someone by my side again, but I don't ever want to be bound again."

Faye nodded. "I guess all the Fighters have that in common."

"Yes," Phoenix said. "The bond can kill us, as you know. It's nothing more than poison after all, and that's the last thing I want in my system."

Nightmare, the leader of the Fighters, entered the gathering room.

She tensed. She'd never get used to the dark bastard. He was handsome, with black hair, a tall muscular frame, and biceps as big as her thighs, but everything about him screamed *"stay away"*. The cold and always angry look in his eyes didn't ease the impression.

Faye cringed. She didn't doubt he could snap her in two

without breaking a sweat if he wanted to. What was MedAct thinking when they created cyborgs like him? Nightmare approached and looked straight at her. "He's ready for you."

She held her breath for two seconds as blood rushed to her face.

His gaze narrowed. "You're not chickening out, are you?"

She stood and licked her lips. "I only said I'd talk to him, nothing more."

He studied her for what felt like hours, then sighed. "You really have no idea what you've gotten yourself into, do you? Do you really believe you can walk in there and just *talk* to him? I've had him tied to the wall with chains to make sure he won't hurt you, because believe me, that's what he wants to do."

Faye took a step back. Even if she tried to be nice and relaxed in front of the Fighters, she was still tense on the inside, especially when Nightmare was around.

They were the Fighters, after all, viewed as dangerous, unpredictable, and untrustworthy by the outside world.

Phoenix stood. "Cut it out, Nightmare."

The leader snorted. "I'm being honest."

"You can be honest in a different way."

His gaze darkened. "She brought this on herself, so don't start that shit. If she hadn't kissed Silver, she wouldn't be here."

"If I hadn't kissed him, Shade would've been beaten senseless." She kept her voice cold, and she glared at the Fighters' leader. She didn't care who he was, or how

11

dangerous he was.

If he tried anything, she'd fight back, no matter how scared she was.

Nightmare gave her a once-over. "For someone as small as you, you sure have a lot of spirit."

Faye straightened her back. "You don't scare me."

Something wicked awakened in his shining eyes. "You're a terrible liar." He took a step closer, invading her personal space. "I know I do. I see it in your eyes, but I'm nothing compared to what awaits you."

She licked her lips, trying to remain calm, but her heart thundered like crazy. "What're you talking about?"

"You're the last person Silver wants to see, and he hates what you've done to him."

That actually hurt, but she bit her lip to stop the emotions from coming over her. "And he's the last person *I* want to see, but somehow, we have to get through this, so you better stop talking bullshit, and take me to the son of a bitch."

Silence filled the gathering room.

All the Fighters had their gazes fixed on her and Nightmare. None of them looked worried. Instead, they seemed ready for a fight, as if it was nothing new.

Faye barely dared to look away from the tall leader, even if she felt her gaze flicker, but looking away meant showing weakness, and showing herself as lesser in front of this bastard was the last thing she'd ever do.

She didn't doubt, that in Nightmare eyes, she was nothing more but an annoying bug. Compared to him, she

12

was tiny, with her slim form and height of five foot two. He towered over her like a dark shadow that refused to back away.

Self-confidence suddenly hit her, and she put her hands on her hips, giving him a grin. "If you keep staring like that, a girl might get the wrong idea, but I guess you just find me attractive enough to keep looking." She snorted when he didn't flinch. "Maybe I should kiss you too and see if I can bind you to me as well. After all, my bond to Silver isn't sealed yet."

That did it.

Nightmare backed away.

Faye couldn't bind him to her, and he knew it too, but it was obvious the rogue cyborg wouldn't take any chances. She'd hugged several Fighters. There wasn't anything wrong with that, and without initiating another bond. Kissing them would be completely different though, and who knew, maybe that *could* initiate a bond.

Irritation shone in Nightmare's eyes. "My need for a woman is so great you can't even imagine how great. I passed my limit a long time ago, and like most Fighters, I hang on a thin thread. Why do you think so many of us are locked up? Because the bond has driven them crazy, so stop your teasing, because before you know it, I might take you up on it…or one of them."

She bit down and looked around.

All the Fighters still watched her, and for the first time since she'd come there, she saw them for who they were.

Starved men who hungered for affection.

If any of them gave in to the bond, they'd jump her.

One Fighter's gaze especially filled her with deep worry. He was slimmer and shorter than most of them but seemed to have difficulties standing still. He shifted foot to foot, glaring with a determination that made Faye flinch.

She'd never spoken to him, but his name was Edge. She'd tried to say hello a few times, but he'd always avoided her.

Faye also recognized him from the abandoned house where Nightmare had tried to remove Shade's bond to Phoebe.

"Do you understand now, Faye?" Nightmare asked, and she met his gaze. "You're not safe here."

"You wouldn't hurt me." Her voice broke.

"No, none of us would. Not voluntary, but you and Celise are the first women who've come close to us. Before you two, no woman has ever sat a foot down here. You being here doesn't make the need easier to handle. Our bonds still see you as a potential bound one since your bond to Silver isn't set. Celise's safe, but you won't be until your bond with Silver is sealed."

Phoenix and Sense took a step closer.

"Don't worry," Phoenix said. "Nightmare's just trying to freak you out. Yes, we all desire a new bound one, but we can control the need. Those who can't are locked up."

His words eased some of her tension, and she looked at the rogue leader with new self-confidence. "I thought you were going to take me to Silver, instead of having this

14

nonsense-filled conversation."

He snorted. "Believe what you want." He headed for the door. "Follow me."

Faye swallowed and hesitated.

Phoenix grabbed her arm. "Don't worry. I'll go with you."

She smiled. "Thank you."

Sense remained as they followed Nightmare.

No one spoke, but Faye could swear they heard her heart pounding.

The last time she'd seen Silver was in the abandoned house, and she had no idea what to expect now.

The bond wasn't real. Wind proved that yesterday when he explained what he'd gone through after Diane's death. Apparently, the bond was nothing more but a poison, designed to kill a cyborg as his bound one died, and Faye still had a hard time processing everything.

If it failed, the cyborg survived and joined the Fighters, but the bond never stopped screaming for a new bound one. It drove some of the Fighters mad. The ones she'd seen had been sane enough, but at the same time, she'd never seen any of the Fighters who were locked up.

Nightmare had said there were about fifty of them, and over thirty had to be taken away; restrained. Those were not promising numbers.

It'd been days, weeks, since she'd seen Silver, and who knew what condition he was in.

She'd kissed him to save Shade, but in a way, the Fighter had it coming.

15

They walked down a wide corridor. It was well lit, the walls painted in white, and the floor was in stone. Everything about this place reminded her of a hospital, with its clean and bright environment.

Faye and the two Fighters passed several closed doors that Nightmare opened with his handprint or digital keys.

The further they went, the more she felt like she was walking into a prison. "How far does these hallways go?"

"For miles," the leader answered, "but don't worry. We have them all covered. No one can enter our home without us knowing. After all, I've had years to build this place, and when others started to join me, it became easier."

A loud bang came suddenly from a door they passed.

Faye jumped, and backed into Phoenix as she stared.

The door had a window, and through it, two shining eyes stared right at her. They belonged to an attractive cyborg with model-like features, but it was impossible to miss the madness lingering in the glow peering out.

"Who the hell is that?"

Nightmare gazed toward the locked-up cyborg. "His name's Sphere, but don't worry. He can't get out."

She swallowed and studied the Fighter.

Those eyes never left her. It seemed like he wanted to devour her, and something told her he'd hurt her if he got his hands on her.

He probably wouldn't mean it, but something told her he had no control over his actions, judging by the bruises on his face and his dark hair that probably hadn't seen a comb in forever.

"What's wrong with him?"

"His mind is lost," Nightmare said. "Some of us react worse than others to the loss of the bond. Sphere was one of them. Honestly, the kindest thing would be to put him out of his misery."

Faye's jaw dropped. "The kindest thing? I can't believe you just said that."

The leader raised an eyebrow. "Take a close look at him and tell me what you see."

She licked her lips and glanced at the Fighter. "Pain."

"Exactly. He's in a lot of pain. The day before we met Celise, we decided to end his life because he wasn't improving, but now that she's in the picture, I see hope for him. When she and Wind come back in a few days, I'll let her take a look at him. Now let's move on." He kept walking. "Silver's waiting for you."

CHAPTER 3

When Nightmare stopped in front of a door and met her gaze, a cold chill traveled down Faye's spine.

"Is this where—?"

He nodded. "Remember what I told you, he's tied up. Silver won't be able to hurt you, but I can't keep him tied forever. I *will* have to let him go eventually."

Phoenix's gaze darkened. "I don't like this."

"You don't have to," Nightmare said. "She has to do this, whether she wants to or not. I will not lose Silver." His gaze landed on her again. "Bind him to you. Once we figure out how to remove the bond, both of you will be set free."

She crossed her arms. "What if I refuse?"

The leader snorted. "Do you really believe I'll let you go if you refuse? His life is in your hands. *You* chose to kiss him. Without you, he'll die, so take responsibility for your actions, and bind him to you." He pressed his hand against the plate next to the door and a click sounded. "I'll leave the door open so you can get out, but I'll also give you a few hours to make sure the second flash happens. It shouldn't take much since his bond is screaming for it. After that, I'll release him. It'll be up to you if he'll be calm by then or not."

Phoenix's shoulders tensed. "I'll stay here, and make sure she's safe."

Nightmare nodded. "Good." He left without saying another word.

Faye couldn't tear her eyes off the door. Knowing Silver was behind it made her shiver all over. She wanted nothing more but to run away.

This was the last place she wanted to be, but she'd chosen to stay.

Somehow, she'd get through this.

Everything inside her screamed to not bind Silver to her, but what other option did she have? None, really.

Maybe doing what Nightmare wanted *was* the only way, and it didn't sound *that* bad. She could bind Silver to her, and afterward, they could stay away from each other until Celise and the others had come up with a way to remove the bond.

Faye doubted the cyborg wanted anything to do with her, and he'd probably be happy with that solution. Besides, she didn't want his death on her conscience.

"I'll be here," Phoenix said. "Just yell if you need me, and I'll be in the room within a second."

She nodded and smiled, grateful for him wanting to protect her. If anything went wrong, she'd be hopeless. A cyborg was a lot stronger than a human, and an angry cyborg was nothing to play around with.

Faye took a deep breath to calm herself. It did no good, because when she put her hand on the door handle and pulled it down, her heart went into a frenzy. She had no idea what to expect when she opened the door. Silver was tied to the wall. That meant he wouldn't be able to reach her if she stayed close to the door ... hopefully.

Memories flooded her when she went inside.

She'd never had much interest in cyborgs, but from what she could remember, Silver was one of the hottest ones she'd ever seen; a body to die for and with a cocky gaze in his aluminum-colored shining eyes.

They'd done nothing but argue ever since they'd met, but he'd also flirted with her, and Faye had flirted back. It had been exciting and arousing because every time he'd given her that wicked grin, her body had reacted. Her sex had clenched with need, and it'd made her curse her lonely existence.

Every guy she'd dated over the years had turned out to be a pain in the ass. They were the reason to why she'd been on her own the past three years.

She'd focused on her career instead. Running two companies, in design and marketing, had given her enough money to buy a home in Glaswell.

It was *her* fault she and Silver were in this situation, but if the Fighters hadn't tried to hurt Shade, she would've never kissed Silver. The only thing that tormented her was the pain she'd put him through.

Now, Faye was here to set them both free.

The room she entered was small, white, and only contained a bed and a toilet that could be hidden with a curtain, but none of that mattered when she met Silver's wild gaze.

He stood with his back to the wall with his arms chained to it by his wrists.

She froze and stared. The fury in his shining eyes almost made her regret coming. She squeezed the door handle.

It surprised her how intense the shine in his eyes was, it was almost blinding, but he was just as handsome as she remembered, despite his messy blond hair and flushed cheeks. A thin coat of sweat covered his skin and his wrists were red.

Faye frowned. Had he been trying to set himself free?

Silver flashed his teeth. "Leave. Leave now."

She remained, stuck to her spot, then took a deep breath and stepped inside the room, closing the door behind her. "Nice to see you too, Silver." His name felt like candy on her tongue. For some reason, she liked saying it.

He pulled on the chains hard, making her jump.

She'd never seen anyone as pissed as he was right now. It made her tense; ready to flee.

The tiny cracks in the walls around the chains whispered of his strength, and so did his muscular frame.

21

Her memory hadn't been wrong. The sight of his appealing body made her lick her lips. Then, she cursed. He *still* had that effect on her, but Faye didn't want to be attracted to him.

She was here to set them both free, nothing else.

She'd sleep with him if she had to, to set the bond, but that was it. Faye sat on the bed and gave him a self-assured smile she didn't feel on the inside. "I guess you know why I'm here."

"If you touch me, I'll kill you."

The threat was no joke.

She sighed and stood. Maybe coming here had been the wrong move after all. "Then I'll just leave you here to rot." She headed for the door.

Obvious panic filled Silver's glowing eyes. "No." He gasped.

Faye crossed her arms like she had earlier. "You really don't know what you want, do you?"

He shook his head, as if to shake something off him. "It's my bond talking. It wants you to finish what you started."

Even if he was pissed, the pain and exhaustion was easy to spot. It was written all over his face, and she didn't doubt the bond was slowly driving him crazy.

She'd gained enough information about it to understand how it behaved.

It probably screamed inside him like a madman, and now when she was here, in front of him, it frustrated the hell out of him. She was so close, and yet so far away.

In a way it made her feel powerful. Faye literally held his life in her hands. "And what do you want?" she asked.

"Take one wild guess," he hissed.

She snorted and dared to take two steps closer. "Let's make one thing clear. I don't want to be here. I've no interest in you, *whatsoever,* but I'm here because I have a conscience." The not-wanting-him-part wasn't exactly true, but *he* didn't need to know that. "Honestly, you had this coming. If you Fighters hadn't touched Shade, none of us would've been in this situation. I can walk away and never look back, but that means you'll die." She looked him over. "I see you're hurting, but you want as little to do with me as I want with you." Faye swallowed so she wouldn't falter. "Therefore, I think we should just do this, and we can stay out of each other's ways until the Fighters and Celise know how to remove the bond."

Silver remained silent for a moment, and then he started laughing.

Faye blinked. "What's so funny?"

"You really are naïve. Do you really believe you can bind me to you and *walk away*? My instincts to be by your side will be over the roof. My bond will make sure the only thing I'll want is to stay by your side, protect you, and love you. But do you really think that's what *I* want?" His gaze darkened. "Bond me to you, and I'll protect and love you, but I'll hate you for it for as long as I'll live."

She stood paralyzed. The hate in his gaze was unmistakable, and it slowly killed her on the inside.

Maybe she'd been wrong.

Maybe all the flirting and teasing had been nothing but a game for him. Maybe she'd imagined the tiny hint of interest she'd seen in the abandoned house.

Maybe he really *did* hate her.

She didn't move. Uncertainty dominated, but then anger grabbed her, and it filled her to a level she'd never experienced before. Faye slapped his cheek hard.

The hit threw his head to the side, and he groaned.

"You want to die? Be my guest. I don't give a fuck about you." She stormed out of the room, not missing the surprise in Silver's eyes.

A roar of despair filled the air as she slammed the door behind her.

Phoenix gave her a worried look. "That sounds like it didn't go so well."

She took a deep breath, trying to calm her nerves. "He's a bastard. Even if I don't want any of this, I really did try."

His lips twitched. "True. He's a bastard, and I don't like him very much, either, but deep down, he has a heart … probably … somewhere."

Faye couldn't help but smile.

Phoenix had a calming effect on her. Why couldn't it have been *him* she'd kissed? He would've been a lot easier. He was handsome, with his unique and androgynous appearance, but she felt no attraction toward him. That was sad, because he seemed like the perfect guy.

Despite how Silver had reacted to her presence, she still

couldn't get away from wanting to help him, but another part of her wanted to walk away and never look back.

His words had hurt like hell, and the last thing Faye needed in her life was a cyborg that would always despise her.

She didn't doubt his words. He *would* love her and take care of her, but he'd also never forgive her for forcing him into a new bond. In a way, he was already stuck in it.

Just like her.

"Are you going to go back in there?" Phoenix asked.

Faye nodded. "I don't have much of a choice, do I? Nightmare will be furious if I don't bond Silver to me, and Silver will be furious if I do it, so I guess I'll go with what Nightmare wants me to do. He's way scarier than Silver. Silver's just pissed."

Phoenix touched her arm and gave her a reassuring look. "Don't let Nightmare get to you. He might be big and scary, but he means well."

She frowned. "He sure has a strange way of showing it."

"He's not as bad as you might think. The media really does have a wrong image of him, but at the same time, you must understand he's lived a tough life. His patience is low and he's often angry, but all he wants is to save us all." He shifted his weight to the other leg. "Imagine this. You've known the truth about the bond for over forty years, but no one believes you. No one listens, not until now has someone believed him. Something like that can drive anyone crazy."

Faye blinked. "I've never … thought about it like that before."

"No one has. I'm one of the few who got away easily when my bond tried to kill me. It screams inside me to find a new bound one, but I can handle it. For Nightmare, it's a lot worse. He hides it well, but I see how it's breaking him down little by little every day."

She swallowed. "And Silver?"

He shrugged and grinned. "He's just a mean bastard."

Faye snorted. "I figured."

CHAPTER 4

Silver glared at the door, waiting for it to open again. His chest heaved and sank fast, fury pumping in his veins. He pulled at the chains holding him to the wall, hoping he could set himself free, but all he got was even more protest from the bites in his wrists.

The sweet little blonde couldn't have walked out fast enough. She'd barely spent a minute with him, but when he'd laid his eyes on her, his heart had almost stopped beating.

He'd devoured her small figure and appealing beauty with his hungry gaze as the bond had pounded in his chest, but Faye hadn't noticed.

She'd been too tense, and seconds later, they'd been arguing. His cheek still stung from the slap.

Ever since she'd kissed him in the abandoned house, things had been hell. Things had been hell before then too, but it was nothing compared to now.

His body was in a constant aroused state, his muscles shook with need and frustration. The desire to thrust deep inside her was almost overwhelming.

It was eating him alive on the inside.

Chaos.

That was the right—and only—word to describe what he was going through.

Silver let out a roar of anger, pain, and frustration, yanking the chains again, desperately needing to be free, to find her, and bind himself to her.

He couldn't take it much longer.

He didn't want this, but the bond wasn't giving him much choice. Soon, his mind would shut down, and his primitive instincts would take over. They'd rule him, and the only thing that would matter would be Faye.

He'd find her and make her his.

Silver shook his head. "No," he gasped. "I refuse." He shut his eyes. "I … don't … want … this."

A thin coat of sweat broke out all over his body. His head was spinning, and it was difficult to focus. His bond didn't care what *he* wanted.

Instead, the more he protested, the more it screamed inside him to bond Faye to him.

This was a complete disaster.

A disaster he'd never seen coming.

The door handle went down, and the panel slowly opened.

Silver shot his eyes up. Anticipation filled him.

Had she come back?

Faye walked in with clenched fists. She avoided looking at him at first, then slowly raised her head and met his gaze. There was a mix of insecurity and nervousness there, but at the same time, a hint of interest and excitement.

He pulled at the chains again and she paused; watching him. Maybe she worried he'd get loose and throw himself at her.

Well, there *was* a risk of that.

The chains held him in place, though.

Being locked up filled him with desperation once more. Silver wanted to roar his anger and frustration anew, but that would only scare her away, and he needed her, no matter how much he *hated* it. "Please," he begged. "Kiss me. I can't take this anymore." He really couldn't.

The havoc-ridden emotions the bond created within him from just one look at her, made him almost go crazy.

There would be no turning back once his mind was lost. Not even a kiss would save him.

Only a bullet would end his suffering.

It was a dangerous game she played with him.

And she didn't even know it.

Faye raised an eyebrow. "You think I'm stupid? The last thing I want is to approach you when you look so wild and out of control."

Silver didn't blame her. He probably looked like a big mess. His clothing glued to his skin, his hair hung all over his face, and sweat dripped down his cheek. His heavy breathing didn't make things better.

He needed a second kiss, and she needed to give it to him.

Now.

One kiss, and the pain would ease. He'd get his control back.

Her first kiss had initiated the bond, and with it, a fierce need and desire to bond with her. He needed a second kiss to make his eyes flash again. That would make his programming accept the bond. That was where he'd end things. He'd need a third flash, but he'd be able to live without it.

He hoped.

Faye sat on the bed. She crossed her legs and gave him an irritated glare.

Silver frowned. What was she doing? Didn't she understand that her presence was pure torture, especially when she kept her distance?

He pressed his jaws together. Had to try to stay calm. That was the only way she'd ever dare to approach him. The last thing he needed was Faye leaving the room again.

He wouldn't be able to handle it a second time.

"Let's talk," she said.

Silver cursed on the inside. What the hell did she want to *talk* about in a moment like this? "About what?" He somehow managed to ask without shouting.

"Tell me about yourself."

He winced. "Why do you want to know things about me?"

Faye shrugged. "I figured I should know something about the cyborg I'm about to bind to me."

Silver clenched his fists. "I was created and bound to a woman called Claire Adams. I lived with her for several years, she died about a year ago, I joined the Fighters, and here we are. Happy?"

She snorted. "You think you're funny?"

"I'm in a little bit of a hurry."

"If you want me to kiss you, you better answer my questions first."

Silver cursed even louder on the inside. "Then ask them."

Faye licked her lips, insecurity crossed her eyes. "Were you happy?"

What kind of question was that? "Of course, I was happy. Has there ever been a cyborg who wasn't? As long as she lived, everything was fine, but the moment her life ended, my world collapsed. All Fighters share the same story, and all cyborgs share the same fate. Sooner or later, the bound one *will* die, and we will remain if we survive. That's one of the reasons why the bond needs to be eliminated."

She licked her lips again and grabbed the linens before shifting slightly on the bed.

Silver frowned. Was she nervous?

"What was she like?" Faye asked.

He sighed. Memories of his beautiful Claire filled him. She, who always had a smile for everyone, and a gentleness in her big brown eyes that made everyone trust her. He'd loved her with pure devotion, but he'd also been blind to the reality around him. It wasn't until he'd met Nightmare and the other Fighters that he'd understood why he'd almost died with her.

"Claire was an outgoing and loving woman. She was everybody's friend, and no one ever seemed to think lesser of her."

Faye blinked. "That doesn't sound like a woman who'd create a cyborg like you."

Silver snorted. "I haven't always been like this. Back then, I was more like her, but she wanted a cyborg who'd flirt and tease. Someone who was just as outgoing as she was. Someone who'd enjoy life to the fullest."

She swallowed. "What did she do for a living?"

"She was a freelance journalist, so we traveled a lot. Those were amazing times." He took a deep breath. Warmth filled his heart when he remembered Claire's smiling face. The way she used to look at him always made him feel as if nothing mattered more than him.

Faye's deep sigh brought him back to reality.

His bond to Claire was since long gone. He desired Faye now. Not by choice, but there was nothing he could do about it. All he wanted was this hell to end. The torment was almost worse than what he'd gone through when he'd lost his bound one, probably because it had gone on for so long now.

"How did she die?" Faye wondered.

When was she going to stop asking him questions?

He needed her to kiss him!

Now!

"She got shot while she interviewed a man. I saw it happen, but I was too far away to prevent it. She died a few days later in the hospital, and I died with her." He glared harder when he spotted sadness in Faye's eyes. The last thing he needed was *her* pity.

"I'm sorry."

"Don't worry about it. I woke up in MedAct a few days after with Jade by my side. She claimed to do everything in her power to save me, but I'd realized what the bond really was. Somehow, I barely remember how I managed to escape. Nightmare found me and saved me with that little signal of his."

"You mean the signal he put in Wind to block his old bond from trying to kill him?"

Silver nodded. "Exactly. It helped me, until *you* kissed me. Now my bond is in havoc because of you."

She straightened her back. "Well, you had it coming."

Faye seemed to refuse to look him in the eyes, and if she did, it only lasted a few seconds before she looked away again.

She wasn't behaving as he remembered her. Where had that brave and forward little Faye gone? She seemed more nervous than ever.

It didn't matter. Right now, he just wanted that damn kiss.

A heaviness was starting to fill his head, and a headache wasn't far away. The way his heart pounded worried him. It hurt, and not in a good way.

Faye looked down. "I guess Claire and I have nothing in common."

"No, you don't."

She clenched her fists, and it was impossible to miss the hurt in her eyes.

Realization hit him, and he grinned. "Oh, I see. Don't tell me you've fallen for me? That's why you're asking about Claire?"

Her gaze shot to his. She stared with wide eyes and an open mouth. Her fingers trembled.

Silver widened his grin. "Don't worry, sweetheart. I'll be madly in love with you soon. You just have to kiss me." He pouted with his lips and made a kissing sound. "Come here. I'm waiting."

Faye flew to her feet. "You son of a—"

He raised an eyebrow. "What? Am I wrong?"

"You really believe I'm asking about your late bound one because I've fallen for you? I wanted to get to know you."

His grin shifted to an irritated glare. "You can get to know me later. Right now, I'm really craving that kiss, you know." The pain in his chest increased and it felt like a miracle Silver hadn't died from the pressure his body was put through yet. His mind started to fog.

The room was spinning, and something told him he only had minutes left.

All thanks to *her* being here.

Near, but far away…

A glimpse of worry crossed Faye's gaze. "You look sick."

He wished he could dry away the sweat on his forehead. "It's the bond. It's tearing me apart on the inside, longing for you…so badly…"

She remained silent for what felt like an eternity, just studying him, then she moved closer.

Anticipation awakened within him.

"Fine." She grabbed his face. "But if you try to bite me, you'll regret it."

He couldn't hold back the gasp that left his mouth when she entered his personal space. His bond instantly started to scream. The craze from before was nothing compared to what it put him through right now.

Her gentle fingers pressed against his cheeks, and Faye looked him straight in the eyes. She slowly opened her mouth and tilted her head slightly to the side as her gaze turned to his lips.

His body started to tremble.

Her touch awakened a need greater than what he'd ever felt before.

He loved it.

He hated it.

In the end, it didn't matter what he felt. It was all the bond's doing. It controlled him, controlled his feelings and needs.

There was no other way but to bind himself to Faye.

Only if Celise and Nightmare managed to figure out how to remove the bond would he finally be free.

Silver didn't miss the insecurity that shone right through her. Did she dislike this just as much as he did?

It was hard to tell. Faye had said she wanted nothing to do with him, but her body language spoke another story.

It was impossible to miss the tiny piece of interest in her eyes, but maybe he was mistaken. Maybe it was just insecurity.

He hoped it was. There was no future for them, no matter how much he'd soon love her.

She inhaled and pressed her lips to his.

Every muscle in his body instantly tensed. Silver pulled at the chains and pushed himself closer. The need was too great for him to care about anything anymore. He just wanted the pain to go away.

The sweet scent of her warm skin filled his nose, intoxicating and calming the bond. Her nearness was exactly what the bond wanted.

Her soft lips felt like pure heaven as he claimed them, demanding more. Another type of need grabbed ahold of him. A need to make the second flash happen.

Faye didn't disappoint. She responded, pushing her tongue inside his mouth, claiming him instead, kissing him with eagerness and passion, and he couldn't help but smile.

His feisty little bound one sure knew what she wanted.

Silver winced.

His feisty little bound one?

Already?

He cursed. This was going to be a long week.

Heat started to build up in his eyes. The flash was seconds away.

The bond was responding, and not a moment too late, Silver interrupted the kiss; turned his head away to not blind Faye.

The heat intensified, and he let out a deep groan as his eyes flashed. Relief washed over his whole body as the agony faded away. His muscles relaxed, and for a short moment, his mind went blank.

He had no grasp of how much time had passed when reality grabbed him again.

Silver leaned his head against her shoulder. The pain was gone, but he was exhausted. His body was warm, sweaty, and ached all over. "Oh, thank God," he mumbled.

Faye didn't move. Instead, she put her palm against his chest.

He shivered. He'd never imagined it'd feel *this* good to be touched again, even if the one touching him was Faye. Her gentle fingers were like the sweetest drug.

"Better?" she asked.

Silver groaned again, closing his eyes and just allowing his muscles to relax even more. "You've no idea."

Moments passed, neither of them spoke.

Silver was grateful for these few minutes in peace. He needed it, and something told him he'd sleep for days once Nightmare released him.

Thankfully, the bond remained quiet. Usually, he'd be craving sex now to seal it, but his exhaustion was complete, and maybe the bond sensed that.

His knees trembled. They'd give in soon, but Faye supported him with her small frame as his body leaned heavily against hers.

She groaned. "What're you doing? I can't hold you. You need to stand."

"I can't," he murmured. "I'm so tired." Somehow, he managed to turn his head and inhale her scent. It was amazing and filled every part of him. For a split second, it felt like he was home.

Then, darkness claimed him.

CHAPTER 5

Faye groaned when Silver's heavy body went slack in her arms. Desperately, she tried to hold him up. If she'd let go, he'd be hanging by his wrists because of the chains. He could dislocate his shoulders, and he didn't need more pain. "Phoenix!"

The door flew open and the cyborg entered with wide eyes. He stopped in his tracks, took in the scene, and hurried to her side, grabbing Silver.

She exhaled when his weight eased from her. "Thanks."

"What happened?" Phoenix held him up with ease.

"I kissed him, and he just went out."

He looked peaceful in his sleep, but his messy hair and sweaty face spoke of how much he'd been through these past few weeks.

Guilt filled her. It was all *her* fault. Faye straightened her back. Yes, it *was* her fault, but it was Silver's fault as well. She wouldn't allow this to pray on her anymore.

Footsteps filled the hallway outside the room.

Nightmare entered. The Fighters' leader raised an eyebrow, studying them before grinning. "Well, I see everything turned out well." He took a keychain from his pocket and approached. "Let's remove the chains."

He released Silver, and together with Phoenix, they lay him on the bed.

Silver didn't stir.

Faye watched her would-be cyborg. That was all she could do. A part of her wanted to help him further, but she'd done what she'd come for.

Hopefully, Silver wouldn't need the third and final flash, but deep down, a voice whispered he would.

She sighed. Kissing him again had sent butterflies through her. Being near him had done the same, even if she didn't trust him one bit.

He was just as feisty and cocky as she was.

"Now what?" Faye asked.

Nightmare checked Silver, and after a short moment, straightened to his full height. "He's asleep. The kiss did him good. We should just let him rest."

She licked her lips. "Can I go home now?"

The leader's gaze shot to her. "Go home?" His eyes darkened. "Don't start with me again. I'm sure you're smarter than you look and know very well that the *last* thing you can do is go home."

Faye opened her mouth to protest but closed it.

He was right. She couldn't go home, even if it was what she wanted most. Getting even more involved with Silver wouldn't end well. Did she really want him in her life?

Maybe some small part of her did, but she doubted anything good would come out of it.

She shrugged. "Whatever."

Nightmare went cold. "Go back to your room. I'll make sure Silver's taken care of until he wakes up, but be ready. He'll come for you once he opens his eyes."

Nervousness swept over her and she swallowed. An image of a barbaric Silver with messy hair and naked torso crossed her mind.

Faye saw him throwing her over his shoulder and carrying her away to his room to have his way with her.

She'd heard how primitive newborn cyborgs were, and since this bond was new to Silver, she doubted he'd be any different.

He'd have only one thing on his mind.

Faye sighed.

There really was no way out of this bond.

Silver still lay where he'd been placed, unmoving. His handsome face was peaceful, and it made funny things to her lower parts.

She really enjoyed watching him. His full lips and strong jawline were exactly what she found attractive in a man.

When his eyes had flashed, and he'd made that deep groan, she'd gasped. The sound had awakened every nerve ending in her body, making her tremble with need.

"Maybe it's best if I stay here and wait for him to wake up. That way, he won't have to run around looking for me," Faye told Nightmare.

The leader frowned. "Do you intend sitting in here for a few days?"

She winced. "What?"

"He'll be out for days. Silver's body has been put through so much, it'll take some time for him to wake up. You can ask Blaze if you doubt me, but he'll tell you the same thing." He glanced at Silver. "Besides, it'll be dangerous for you. Who knows how he'll behave. Worst case scenario, he'll be out of his mind."

Faye swallowed again. "So, what do you want me to do?"

"Nothing. Stay in your room and stay away from the Fighters. Don't try making friends. They might seem friendly, but eventually, one, or several of them, might snap and take you against your will, and that's the last thing you want, right?"

She clenched her fists. Staying in her room for several days sounded like a complete, well, nightmare. She couldn't stay in one place for too long without going crazy. She needed air, but being in her room sounded better than being attacked. "Fine."

Nightmare raised an eyebrow. "You're not going to fight with me?"

"No."

He snorted and grinned. "I'm kind of disappointed. I was almost looking forward to a yelling match with you."

Faye didn't find his attitude amusing—in the slightest. "I can fulfill your wish if you want me to."

The leader grabbed her arm. "Don't even think about it." Nightmare dragged her out of the room.

Phoenix followed without a word.

CHAPTER 6

Faye paced near the elevator with her arms behind her back, waiting for it to come down. Wind and Celise would be there in moments.

Blaze had gone up to the surface to bring them down.

It'd been three days, and boredom was making her go out of her mind. For once, she'd obeyed Nightmare, and had spent her time reading books, and watching TV in her room.

Food had been brought to her. She hadn't been allowed to eat with the Fighters, and maybe that'd been for the best. Some of the rogue cyborgs enjoyed her company, others held their distance.

Faye had no issues with any of them, but Edge's weird gazes sent cold chills down her spine. She didn't want to be near him, but at least, she hadn't been completely abandoned.

Phoenix and Sense had visited her several times, and they'd spent a few hours talking and laughing, sharing tasty food.

The buzzing sounds from the elevator told her it was on the move. Any second now, she wouldn't be alone anymore.

The elevator finally stopped, and the doors opened.

Wind, Celise, and Blaze exited.

The redheaded medic cyborg had a wide smile on his lips. There even was a spark of excitement in his eyes.

Was he happy to see Celise again?

"Finally!" Faye jumped her friend, hugging her hard.

Celise winced but smiled. "Happy to see me?"

"Oh, you have no idea! It feels like I've been here for years."

Her friend gave her a once-over. "Well, you seem to have been well taken care of."

Faye gave her a once-over too, and grinned.

Celise cheeks had a healthy glow, and her eyes sparkled. Her cute and heart-shaped face was full of life. Her blonde hair hung down her shoulders, and she even had some makeup on, something she usually didn't wear.

"You too. I see Wind has a positive influence on you."

She blushed and cleared her throat.

Faye's gaze turned to her friend's new cyborg.

Wind's shiny eyes watched her, and even if she noticed a tiny pinch of sadness in them, he seemed fine. His brown hair was in a ponytail, and he wore a simple T-shirt, and jeans. He held a bag that he held out to her. "Here, we brought you the things from your house that you wanted."

Faye took the bag. "Thanks. I can't wait to change clothes."

Phoenix had offered her some of his clothing, but she'd turned it down. Somehow, that'd felt way too intimate, and Silver would probably not appreciate the gesture. So, to save her cyborg friend's life, she'd said no.

"How are things going with Silver?" Celise asked as they walked down the hallway toward Blaze's infirmary.

She licked her lips. "Well. Things are rather boring right now. He's been asleep for the past three days."

The doctor frowned. "Three days?"

Faye nodded. "He's been out since I kissed him."

Her friend's eyes widened. "That sounds rather worrisome. I think I should take a look at him."

"Don't worry," Blaze said. "I'm checking him several times each day. He's fine, just exhausted to the point that his system has shut down. He needs to regenerate, and that might take some time. After all, ever since Faye kissed him, he's been under more pressure than any cyborg before him. I've never heard of an unfinished bond before."

Wind nodded. "Activating the bond did that to him, without a doubt, especially since he didn't get his mad frenzy satisfied at once."

Faye crossed her arms over her chest. "Don't try to blame me for it."

The medic cyborg's gaze shot to her. "No one's blaming you, but Nightmare would've if Silver had died. At least you

46

saved him from that, but the bond is still not sealed. One more flash to go."

She rolled her eyes. "Don't remind me."

"I still want to take a look at him," Celise said. "You've said it yourself, Blaze, cyborgs aren't your expertise. Where's he now?"

Blaze only nodded. "As you wish. He's in the infirmary. We transferred him there just in case."

"Good."

"There's another Fighter we'd like you to examine, as well."

"Of course. What's wrong with him?"

The medic's lips pursed. "We don't know. Nothing's working. Not even Nightmare's signal that blocks the bond seems to be helping."

"I've seen him," Faye said. "His name is Sphere, and he seems completely out of his mind. Nightmare said they were going to end his life, but they changed their minds when you came into the picture."

Anger dashed across Celise's pretty eyes.

Blaze squeezed her shoulder, earning a warning-glare from Wind. He quickly removed his hand but didn't look away from Celise. "There was no other way. He's in a lot of pain, and if you can't find a way to fix him, he'll die, sooner or later."

She sighed. "Let's start with Silver. Wind and I have also examined the information on the portable hard-disk Nightmare gave me. We have a lot to talk about."

CHAPTER 7

The infirmary was white and wide. It was filled with all kinds of machines. There were also three hospital beds, and two cabinets loaded with medicine and necessary medical equipment.

The light was bright, and the room had a hospital feel to it. Everything was fresh, and even a clinical scent filled the air.

Faye tensed when she spotted Silver lying on one of the beds. She hadn't seen him since she'd kissed him, and his striking and masculine beauty had an instant effect on her, awakening goosebumps on her skin.

He seemed to be cared for. His blond hair was brushed, he'd been washed, and had different clothes on. An IV was attached to his arm, making sure he got all the nutrients he needed while he was unconscious.

Nightmare stood by his bed. He raised his head as they

entered the room, and for the first time in days, he smiled, as he spotted Celise.

Faye snorted to herself. Of course, he'd be happy to see the human doctor. She was just as precious to him as any of his Fighters. *She* was the one who was going to help them change everything.

Faye stilled. She suddenly felt like an unnecessary game piece.

"Welcome back," the leader said but didn't approach them. He gave Wind a nod and got one back. "Has everything gone well?"

"Yes," Celise answered and placed her bag on one of the beds.

Nightmare turned to Wind. "And you?"

His face was tight, tense. "I'm fine."

The Fighters' leader studied him. "Just like that? Don't you miss your late bound one?"

Wind's gaze darkened. "I do, but that's not something I wish to discuss with you. We've buried her and are moving on. Let's do what we came here for." He was cold as he glared at Nightmare, and Faye didn't blame him.

They would probably never get along, and neither would *she* and Nightmare.

The Fighters' leader had planned to use Wind if his experiment on Shade would've failed. Thankfully, he never got the chance.

Celise took a small device from her bag and approached Silver.

Faye recognized it. It was the scanner used on cyborgs to determine their level of health and functioning. It was black with a screen on one side, and a metallic plate on the other. Faye moved closer to the bed. "Can I help?"

Celise blinked. "You want to?"

"Yes. I want to be useful."

Her friend relaxed and smiled. "I can teach you how to use the scanner, for starters."

Joy filled her. "That sounds great!"

"Is that really necessary?" Nightmare didn't look the slightest pleased.

Celise glanced at him. "Wind and I've studied the information on the hard-drive you gave me, and trust me; we're going to need all the help we can get. Besides, Faye's talented with anything she puts her hands on."

"I don't trust her." His voice was dark.

Celise's expression hardened. "But *I* do, and you're just going to have to trust my judgment."

Faye grinned. She had no idea where the doctor got her strength from, but she liked it. Faye doubted anyone had ever put Nightmare in his place before.

He remained still, but it was impossible to miss his frustration.

It almost felt like she'd just won a competition.

"Let's begin," Celise said. "Faye, remove Silver's shirt."

Her grin instantly died. "What?"

"The scanner needs skin-to-skin contact, and since you're his bound one, it's best for all of us if you're the one touching him in case he awakens."

Sweat broke out on her forehead. "But, I'm not his bound one … yet."

Nightmare sighed. "Stop denying it. It's not going to help you, *or* him. You're his bound one whether you want to be, or not. You became his bound one the moment you kissed him."

Faye swallowed. Breathing was suddenly difficult. "But, what if he wakes up and jumps me?"

"Don't worry. There are three cyborgs in here, and we'll stop him from harming you," Wind said with a smile.

She swallowed again, but relaxed. He'd always had a calming effect on her. "Fine." With shaky hands, she pulled down the blanket from Silver's upper body. A breath got stuck in her throat as she stared at the attractive cyborg in front of her.

He was a masterpiece with his strong jawline, well-defined brows, and high cheekbones. A masterpiece she could stare herself blind on.

"Today, please," Nightmare growled.

Faye jumped from his sudden protest, but instead of arguing, she reached for Silver's T-shirt.

The warmth from his muscular body instantly hit her skin as her fingers grazed him.

Why was she reacting like this? She wasn't supposed to like him, damn it!

He was just a cyborg she had to bind to herself for a while. Hopefully, it wouldn't take too long before they'd be free from each other, but who knew.

Worst case scenario, they'd be stuck together for years.

She gasped when her sight was filled with the intensity of Silver's muscular and fit chest. Her insides clenched, awakening a tormented longing within her. It was almost impossible to stop herself from touching and licking him all over, but somehow, she managed to keep her dignity.

"Yes, we know he's good-looking," Nightmare said with a glare. "Can we please move on?"

She narrowed her eyes. "You're awful."

"Nothing new, sweetheart."

What was going on with her? Usually, she'd be shouting at Nightmare by now, but something stopped her. When she looked at Silver, she just didn't care about ending up in unnecessary discussions.

Instead, she took the scanner from Celise and placed it on Silver's chest. It activated itself and a blue screen lit up. "What should I do?"

Celise leaned closer. "The scanner is easy to use. It has programmed sequences you can use, depending on what you're going to scan. All you have to remember is the code for each sequence, push it in, and let the device do its thing."

She nodded. "Sounds easy enough."

"The code for a full-body scan is eleven forty-four."

Faye pushed it in, the device beeped and started working.

No one said anything during the whole minute the scanner did its job.

Once it was done, a bunch of numbers showed up on the screen.

Celise studied the screen.

Faye studied it too, but to her, it was gibberish. "What does all this mean?"

"View the information as a blood test. Every number must be within a certain range to be considered normal. Outside the range means something's not right, but everything's fine. I'll teach you later how to read all the numbers."

She smiled, excitement filling her. "I guess I won't have much time for my own business in the future, but I don't mind."

Nightmare looked skeptical. "You'll run away as soon as we'll be able to remove Silver's bond to you."

Anger boiled up and she clenched her fists. Only sheer will stopped her from smacking him. "With or without the bond, I'm staying. You might not like me, but I don't like you either. At least one thing we agree on. It might surprise you that I really want to help. It's obvious something fishy is going on, and I won't just sit around and do nothing."

The rogue leader didn't look the slight bit impressed. Instead, he crossed his arms over his chest. "We'll see."

Celise sighed and grabbed a bottle containing a transparent liquid from her bag. "I'll give Silver some Areldin. It will speed up his recovery." She injected the medicine into his arm and glanced at Blaze. "Here, I doubt you have this in your medicine cabinet. MedAct never gives it away." She handed him the bottle.

The medic cyborg gave her a wide smile. His shining red

eyes sparkled. "Thank you. How do I use it?"

"Five milliliters are enough, and no more than one injection. It gives an adrenalin kick, but without stressing the body, and it's also not addictive. It's perfect for exhausted cyborgs who need fast energy. The effect lasts for a few hours. Just don't use it on humans."

"Got it." He placed the bottle inside one of the cabinets.

"He should wake up soon."

Some part of Faye wanted Silver to wake up. She was … almost excited about it. She grabbed a chair next to the bed and sat, earning a suspicious glare from Nightmare, but she didn't care.

Once Silver opened his eyes, he'd need her, and the least she could do was ease his pain. She'd bind him to herself, and once the binding was over, she'd help Celise with whatever she could. She didn't give a damn what Silver did after, as long as he stayed away.

He'd made his lack of interested in her pretty obvious.

"What do you think about the information on the hard-disk I gave you?" Nightmare asked Celise.

She took a deep breath. "It's impressive. If all of it is true, which I assume it is, it will change everything."

He nodded. "It will."

"That means we have to figure out how to make the signal you used on Shade to work. In its present form, it's dangerous, but if we find the missing component, we'll be able to remove the bond."

Blaze moved closer. "As you know, we've been trying to

find the missing component for a long time. The only one who knew anything about it was Alexander Fleming, and he's been missing for the past fifteen years."

"Yes, and he's likely dead." She looked at Nightmare. "But I believe the answer's staring us right in the face." She grabbed the hard-drive Nightmare had given her. "I believe the answer is right here."

The leader's eyes widened, and he stared with an open mouth.

Faye felt the excitement rise in the air. Could Celise be right? "What do you mean?"

"The female cyborg program," Celise said.

"We've checked it," Wind said. "It's complete. We should be able to create a female cyborg with it."

The doctor nodded. "Once she's activated, we should be able to find the answer within her. Right now, the female cyborg program isn't active. I've searched through it. There's nothing there that can help us get rid of the bond, but in its active form …"

Nightmare blinked. "You want us to create the first female cyborg?"

She smiled. "Yes."

Blaze licked his lips, insecurity shining in his eyes. "How? We don't have the equipment. We don't even know where to search for it."

Celise grinned. "Don't worry. *I* know."

CHAPTER 8

Silver's eyelids felt heavy as bricks. He wanted to open them, but they didn't obey. His body was in no better condition. It was as if something was weighing him down, stopping him from moving, but his mind was slowly coming to.

He had a slight headache, but it was fading. At least he was lying on something soft, probably a bed, instead of being tied to the wall. How he'd gotten there was a mystery, but something told him he'd been out for a long time. Every muscle was stiff and aching.

Although his body was still exhausted, he felt clean and not sticky from sweat. The ache and need for the second flash wasn't there anymore either.

Thank God.

Instead, there was another ache now.

An ache that wouldn't go away any time soon …

The more he became aware of everything, the more his

bond started to act up again. His new bound one had been accepted, but the bond still needed to be sealed, and it wouldn't accept anything else.

Faye.

He needed her.

Where was she?

Someone sat next to him, who, Silver couldn't tell, but he sensed it, and there were other people around him. They were talking, but he had difficulty making out what they were saying.

Something stabbed him in the arm, making him wince, but he was still unable to move. The deep sleep held him in its grip for a moment longer.

A hand touched his arm. It made him inhale, and with some effort, he finally managed to move his head. The touch felt like a comforting embrace, soothing his slowly awakening needs.

With each breath he took, it became easier to focus, and after a long minute, Silver opened his eyes … and looked straight in the eyes of a cautious Faye.

She was the one who held her hand against his arm, and an electric spark jolted through his entire system.

All he could do was stare.

He'd never imagined she'd be this beautiful.

Her long blonde hair hung loosely down her shoulders as her big blue eyes blinked, tempting him with her long lashes and full red lips. When she licked them, his desire ignited.

It didn't matter that she did so due to insecurity. To him, every move she made was seductive, and it filled him with excitement. Silver wanted to be seduced, for her to lay her hands on him, and bring a new level of pleasure.

She was his queen, his Venus, and Aphrodite.

His goddess.

Only *she* could give him what he needed.

Oh, God.

He was so screwed.

Silver noticed movement around him, but didn't pay it any attention—couldn't. His bond demanded closure. It screamed within him, filling him with great lust, making him inhale. Trying to remain sane was an almost impossible task when she was so close.

He had no control. All he could do was obey.

There was nothing else he *could* do.

Without a second thought, he flew to his feet, making her jump, and when he wrapped his arms around her, Faye squeaked.

She pushed at his chest. "What're you doing?" There was anger in her voice.

Silver was too strong for her. She wasn't going anywhere, but he didn't want to hurt her, so he loosened his grip without releasing her. He leaned closer and pressed his face against her neck. He took a deep breath and closed his eyes. Faye's scent was an aphrodisiac he couldn't get enough of. He groaned as the need grew stronger.

"What the hell?" Faye shoved her fists into his chest.

"Let go of me!"

Four hands grabbed him, surprising him, and giving her the chance to get away as they forced him to let go of her.

Horror filled him as he watched her run away.

Silver roared and pulled with all his might, pressing his muscles to the limit, without ever removing his gaze from her. He had to be set free, but the hands holding him didn't let go. He needed to bind himself to her.

Didn't she see that? Didn't she understand?

He filled the room with another roar when she hid behind Blaze.

How dared she hide behind another male?

She belonged to him, not Blaze!

"He can't think straight," a male voice said to his right.

Silver whipped his head toward Nightmare.

The Fighters' leader was holding him, preventing him from going to Faye.

Wind was holding his other arm, helping his leader.

"The bond needs to be sealed," Nightmare said. "Choose, Faye. You either do it now, or I'll need to lock him up again, but that might *kill* him this time."

She licked her lips, yet again from insecurity, but it didn't matter.

To him, she looked so sexy it hurt.

"I recommend sealing it," Blaze said. "Get it over with. It's best for both of you. You can't go on like this forever."

Faye gasped. "Are you kidding me? He'll kill me within seconds. Did any of you miss the wild glare in his eyes?"

"We can tie him down, and let you do all the work," Nightmare said.

Her mouth dropped open. "Are you crazy?"

"It's a solution. Either you come up with one yourself, or I'll do it for you."

Faye stomped with one foot, fisting her hands, and tensed her jaws.

Some part of Silver wanted to stop.

She wasn't ready for him, but the question was, would she ever be?

The bond demanded closure, and honestly, the more he looked at her, the more that was becoming the *only* thing on his mind.

He tried to set himself free from the cyborgs' grips again, his eyes fixed on her.

The object of his desire took a step back. "You need to hold him better, or he'll break free soon."

Wind groaned. "We're trying, but he's strong."

"And we're growing tired," Nightmare said. "He has only one thing on his mind right now, and that's getting to you. With a determination like that, it won't be long before we won't be able to hold him any longer."

Faye grabbed Blaze's arm and pulled him closer. Her eyes were huge, filled with fear.

Silver roared a third time.

How dared she touch Blaze again?

The medic cyborg moved instantly away. "I don't recommend touching me. You're making him angrier. You belong to him, and touching another cyborg is forbidden. He won't hurt you, but I might get a broken bone or two from just being too close to you. He's in a primitive state, and for him to gain control again, you must seal the bond."

She remained where she was, just staring. Ready to flee.

Ready to abandon him.

Silver roared and pulled harder to get free.

"That's it!" Nightmare groaned as he tried to hold him. "Celise, bring that chair here."

From the corner of his eye, Silver saw the doctor obey.

She approached them with the chair the leader had beckoned and backed away just as fast.

"Hold him!" Nightmare ordered Wind as Silver was forced down on the chair. "Blaze, the chains."

"I'm on it."

No! Not again!

Silver pulled harder, as the medic hurried to a drawer and grabbed a couple of heavy chains. He recognized them.

They were used on Fighters who needed medical care but were a danger to themselves or others.

He was just that.

They meant well, but his bond didn't care. The chains would stop him from going to Faye, and *that* was pure torture.

He managed to free one arm with a roar, but Nightmare was on him, grabbing him, forcing his hand behind his back as Wind and Blaze tied the chains around his wrists.

Frustration filled Silver and he let out another roar.

61

"There." The leader exhaled, drying the sweat from his forehead. He glanced at Faye. "You'd better seal the bond. We don't have more time for this bullshit. We need to find a way to delete the bond from all the cyborgs, but instead, I'm here, playing around with this nonsense."

She didn't move, but the anger in her eyes was unmistakable. Her fear was slowly fading away.

"We're leaving," Nightmare went on. "I'd wish you luck, but it's not my thing." He headed for the door.

CHAPTER 9

Blaze and Nightmare left the room.

A big lump filled Faye's throat as the door closed behind them.

Only Wind and Celise remained.

The doctor grabbed her hands. "Don't worry. We won't be far away. Just call if you need us."

She frowned. "You know he can snap my neck before I even get the chance to scream, right?"

Her friend gave her an understanding smile. "He doesn't want to snap your neck, Faye."

Faye snorted. "I'm not sure I like your new attitude."

Celise just kept smiling as she and Wind left the infirmary.

Silence filled the room as the double doors closed behind them.

She slowly turned back to Silver. She swallowed. His

stare was intense.

His starving gaze took her in, and it was like he was devouring her with his eyes.

She tensed but didn't look away. Something about him was different. The cocky Silver seemed hidden away somewhere, but he'd return once the bond was sealed, without a doubt. Right now, the need to seal the bond was overpowering him.

It was written all over his face.

Faye winced when he jerked his arms, but the chains didn't release him. Nightmare, Wind, and Blaze had done a good job.

She relaxed.

Silver wouldn't jump her any time soon.

Faye dared to take a few steps closer. "Are you ... feeling better?"

He studied her for two short seconds. Then he shifted on the chair, pressing his hips upward.

Unintentionally, her gaze lowered to his groin, and she didn't miss the big bulge he was sporting.

Her lower parts clenched from need at the sight.

There really was no way out of this, after all. She had to bind him to her but doing it the Nightmare-way didn't sound too appealing.

Some small part of her had hoped the second flash would've been enough, but it'd only been wishful thinking.

Two would never be enough. He'd be bound to her by now if he hadn't lost consciousness.

"Yeah, I see what's going on with you."

"Come here." His voice was dark.

Faye remained where she was.

Silver inhaled deeply and flashed his teeth. "I won't hurt you."

She snorted. "Really? You look like you want to tear me to pieces."

His breathing became harsher. "It's because I'm so damn aroused it hurts. Only *you* can ease it."

A pinch of guilt filled her, even if she'd promised herself not to feel guilty ever again because of this situation, but it made her move closer.

Her heart thundered. A part of her wanted to run away, but the other part was curious. It wanted to touch him, to explore him, and take her fill of him.

It'd been a while since she'd been with a man, and Silver was one of the most attractive men she'd ever seen.

She wanted him.

But Faye didn't trust him.

Everything about him shouted for her to stay away. His anger killed her desire the most. "I have no idea how I'm supposed to do this. I don't want to take you when you're tied to the chair, but I also don't want to release you. I doubt you'll listen to me or be careful. You'll jump me the first chance you'll get and have your way with me."

His eyes narrowed. "You're my bound one. I'll never do anything to hurt you or go against your wishes."

She frowned. "You expect me to believe that?"

Silver sighed. "I can't go against your wishes when it comes to you and your body, but I can go against your decisions. As my bound one, it's my duty to love you, cherish you, and always be there for you. To always love you and … die for you." The last words left his mouth in a cold bark.

Faye blinked. "I'll never expect you to die for me."

"Well, sorry to disappoint you, sweetheart, but that's part of the bond, whether you like it or not."

Some part of her had simply chosen to ignore it. Faye took a deep breath to calm her nerves. "Look. I never wanted a cyborg. You know why we're stuck in this situation, and let's not turn it into something else. I'll bind you to me, all right? After that, we can … you know … live our lives separately." She winced when the anger in his eyes intensified.

"Just do it," he growled. Silver's chest rose and sank fast, and his forehead glistered from perspiration. His knuckles were fisted, and his lips were a thin line while his shining cyborg eyes were still fixed on her. At least, they weren't shining as intensely anymore.

She didn't doubt this was also putting a lot of strain on him, but she'd hoped, even if she wasn't very fond of him, that the second kiss had somewhat eased his pain. "So … how do you want to do this?" She took a nervous step closer.

He frowned. "Don't tell me you're a virgin."

"What? No. I'm not."

"Good. Then you know how to fuck. Get undressed and help me out of my pants."

66

Faye restrained herself from punching him. Instead, perched her hands on her hips and glared. "If you keep acting this mean, I'll walk out of the room, and you'll be left like this."

Silver snorted. "No, you won't."

No, she wouldn't, but he didn't need to know that.

Besides, Nightmare scared her enough to stay. "You obviously don't know me." She whirled and headed for the door with determined steps.

He gasped behind her. "All right! I'll behave. Just get on with it."

She grinned as she approached again but kept her distance. Faye almost wanted to pet him on the head just to piss him off even more, but she restrained herself. "Fine, but no more touching than necessary." She couldn't believe she'd just said that when all she wanted was to consume him with touches and kisses, but it was for the best.

They had no relationship.

They had nothing.

Only a bond that would be gone soon anyway.

At least, she hoped so. It would be a disaster if it took years for Nightmare and Celise to find the answer.

Worst-case scenario—they would never find it.

She'd be stuck with Silver for the rest of her life. Sure, she was attracted to him, but would she ever be able to fall in love with him?

He'd always love her. Without her love, which was essential, it would slowly destroy him.

Their future looked dark.

And yet …

There was something about him, something that pulled Faye in, allured her to him.

Her fingers trembled as she slowly approached him. Anticipation filled her whole body as she reached for him, and her heart skipped a beat when her hand touched his shoulder.

That part of her that told her to stay away, that he'd hurt her, slowly became more and more silent.

She had to give him a chance, at least *try* to trust him. Silver deserved at least that much from her.

His gaze never left hers as she placed her hand against his cheek, but when he closed his eyes and leaned into her touch, a funny feeling grabbed her.

Faye held back the gasp that wanted to escape her mouth, but she was unable to stop her fingers from trembling.

His complete exhaustion was obvious in his surrendered expression. He didn't want to fight even if he didn't want this. The bond wasn't giving him any other choice.

She could barely imagine what he was going through.

Deep down, it stung. Knowing Silver was falling deeper and deeper in love with her with each flash.

It made her recall what Nightmare had told her several weeks ago in the house where they'd tried to remove Shade's bond to Phoebe.

He'd said Silver would love her deeply, but he would *hate* her for it.

"The feelings are becoming real, aren't they?" Her voice was filled with compassion.

Silver's eyes were still closed, and he kept his head against her hand, as if he couldn't get enough of her touch. "Yes," he mumbled. The fatigue in his voice was deep.

Faye took a breath and nodded.

It was time.

She couldn't postpone this anymore.

With trembling hands, she grabbed her pants and shoved them down her legs, along with her panties. When the air in the room touched her naked skin, she held her breath with a pounding heart. Luckily, her shirt was long enough to hide her sex from Silver's gaze.

His gaze shot to her lower parts. He pulled on the chains, the eagerness in his eyes grew and slowly devoured her.

When he licked his lips, Faye shivered. Some part of her wanted him to lick her instead, to use his tongue on her and bring her to amazing new heights, but nothing like that was going to happen today, or ever.

This was going to be the only time they touched.

After that, they'd go separate ways, bond or no bond.

And yet, her hands twitched, longing to touch him …

She shook her head.

No, she'd only make his eyes flash a third and final time, and that would be it.

"You're really going to do this?" Suspicion lingered in his voice, but his chest rose and sank fast.

"Of course."

Silver raised an eyebrow. "Really? You've been protesting pretty loudly until now."

"I'm taking responsibility." She leaned down and grabbed his belt. "Now, lift your hips."

He didn't object as she unbuttoned his belt and pants.

Faye froze.

She hadn't been with a man for a long time, and Silver was one of the few men that'd made an impression on her, both good and bad.

He was so attractive, with his blond hair, strong face, and shining eyes, that she was almost unable to look away. She just wanted to stare at him, enjoy his beauty, and get her fill of it.

Whoever Claire, his late bound one, had been, she'd created an attractive cyborg with the features of a model. That wicked and teasing gaze in his almond-shaped eyes was just what Faye needed. It'd sparked her interest, and the inner strength he radiated wasn't so bad either.

Right now, she didn't care that he could also be mean and unfriendly. She just wanted him to flirt with her the way he'd done when they met at MedAct for the first time.

She wanted to see his grin again. She wanted his eyes to spark with excitement when he looked at her, but instead, she saw a great mix of anger and passion.

Passion because his bond desired her.

Anger because he was given no other choice.

Her heart clenched. Some part of her ached. Some part of her wanted him to love her … for real.

"What are you waiting for?" Silver's voice was dark and filled with frustration. He moved his hips on the chair, trying to get her to respond.

Faye winced as reality grabbed her, and she pulled down his pants.

His cock instantly jerked straight up, and she stared.

"Wow. You're impressive." She swallowed.

He gave her an angry grin. "I know."

She snorted. There definitely was nothing wrong with his self-esteem.

That made hers spark an inch as she remembered who she had in front of her.

Two could play the game.

Faye leaned down so that they were face to face, looking him straight in the eyes.

Silver leaned closer, most likely impulsively, and aimed for her lips.

She pulled back a few inches. "As little touching as possible, remember?"

He flashed his teeth. "I really don't care right now." He shot forward again, and this time, managed to press his lips against hers before she got the chance to get away.

An instant warm feeling filled her, igniting every nerve ending in her body. The touch of his kiss lingered on her mouth, and it was almost impossible to resist the impulse to wrap her arms around him.

The kiss froze her in place, and when Silver went in for another, she didn't protest.

Couldn't.

It felt too good to feel him this close, to hear him moan as he took what he craved, and all Faye could do was kiss him back.

Silver pulled the chains in an attempt to get free. Maybe he wanted to wrap his arms around her, but she was in no hurry to release him.

The key lay on the table next to them, and it would remain there.

Without breaking the kiss, she straddled him and wrapped her arms around him. She felt the strength in his big muscles.

Cyborgs were a lot stronger than humans, and even if a flinch of fear swept over her, he wouldn't hurt her.

She was his bound one, after all.

His huge body was almost too much, but in a way, she liked it. Faye had just never had anything to do with a man like him before.

He was taller than most human men, and big in every possible way. Even her thighs were smaller than his biceps, and his hands were almost twice as big as hers.

The image of his hands sent a pleasurable shiver through her.

Only imagine what he could do with those hands.

Parting her legs made her feel vulnerable, especially when air hit her sex and his cock grazed her naked skin.

She was more than ready for him and was unable to stop from pressing closer to him.

Faye's fingers tingled. She wanted to open his shirt, enjoy the view of his naked body, and touch him all over, but it was a need she held back.

She'd never felt like this before. Every part of her was filled with excitement, need, and desire. It made her want to forget everything around them, even the reason as to why they were doing this, and just enjoy him.

The rustle of chains filled the room once again, and she didn't miss how tense his muscles were.

Silver's fists were white, but his wrists were red from all the pulling. He moved around on the chair, trying to get her closer to his cock. He panted, almost hissed, and let out a pained groan.

His hunger made her head spin, as he showered her with intense and wet kisses. The shine in his eyes was almost as intense as it'd been before.

Faye knew what it meant.

His bond was waiting for the last and final flash.

He would soon be hers.

Just a little bit more and he'd be bound to her.

Would it be for good?

Hopefully not.

She trusted Celise. Her friend, Nightmare, and Blaze would find the answer. The bond would eventually be removed.

Faye's chest tightened.

Why did that leave an unpleasant feeling in her chest all of a sudden?

She raised her gaze and met his.

Passion was written all over his face and drops of sweat ran down his cheek. Silver even trembled. He couldn't wait anymore. "Do it. Do it now. It feels like I'm going to die if you wait any longer." His voice was raspy, shaky, and filled with need so great it made her throat tighten.

Faye could only nod as she wrapped her small fingers around his cock.

A loud hiss left his mouth and he leaned his head against her shoulder as she gently stroked him. He jerked beneath her, and he twitched in her hand.

It put a smile on her lips as her own sex clenched from need.

The desire to set him free became greater. She wanted nothing more but to have his arms around her, to be under him as he pumped hard and fast inside her.

She wanted to listen to the way he sounded as he filled her, but yet again, she restrained herself. Who knew how he'd behave once she set him free.

Silver seemed gone in his own mind, blinded by his maddening lust.

Faye took a deep breath and raised herself, lingering over his cock for a short moment before she lowered her body, slowly allowing him to enter her.

A moan left her mouth when he stretched her, inch by inch. It hurt a little bit because of his size, but she quickly adapted, and even if his need made him tremble, Silver remained still, allowing her to take her time. She hadn't expected that, but it made her trust him a tiny bit more.

Eventually, she sat on his lap with him filling her completely. She'd never felt this full before. It was an amazing sensation, and she could do nothing but listen to her needs, and slowly start moving on him.

Slowly … up … and down.

He tilted his head back. His eyes were closed, and his mouth slightly open.

It was an erotic sight that made her sex clench, and Faye could no longer hold back the burning inside her.

Time and space disappeared. There was only them, only a passion so high it drove them to new levels.

She held on to him with desperation as her bottom slapped against his legs over and over again.

The sounds of their lovemaking filled the air, and she didn't give a damn if anyone heard them.

Neither did Silver, apparently. He was almost screaming each time she came down on him.

It only drove her desire wilder, and eventually, her body took over.

Her legs started to hurt, but she couldn't stop. She'd have an awful muscle ache once all of this was over, but it'd be so damn worth it. Faye grabbed his biceps and shouted as she came.

Silver trembled beneath her, and a bright light filled the room as he roared.

She felt the heat from his release, and for some reason, she liked it more than she'd expected. She grinned and looked at him.

Sweat covered his forehead, and his breathing was rapid, but he remained still for a long moment, just staring at the ceiling, before he finally met her gaze. He looked just as exhausted as she felt.

His eyes didn't shine as strongly as before. Now, they looked like regular cyborg eyes. "You have really beautiful eyes," she said.

Silver didn't answer. Instead, he rested his forehead against her chest.

Faye winced. She hadn't expected that. "What're you doing?"

"I just need to be close to you for a while." His voice was low and filled with sadness.

"I thought you didn't want that."

"I don't, but my bond does."

She swallowed.

Of course.

She barely dared to move as he pressed himself closer. She didn't doubt he would've wrapped his arms around her if he'd been free.

Faye should move away. They'd agreed to not touch each other, and to stay away from each other once the bond was in place, but some part of her wanted to stay like this.

Feeling the heat of his body against her was soothing. Deep down, it calmed her and made her long for more.

She licked her lips and raised her arms to wrap them around him but froze. Should she?

"Hold me," Silver begged with barely a whisper.

Faye winced again, but did as he asked. Insecurity sang inside her as she placed her arms on his back, not really hugging him, barely touching him. Her heart ached, and tears gathered in her eyes.

Silver's resignation was obvious. He loved her now, but he'd never forgive her for it.

"I should've never kissed you," she said, and her words trembled.

He pressed his cheek closer to her chest. "No, you shouldn't have."

CHAPTER 10

Stepping inside the gathering room left her with a weird feeling, especially when everyone turned and stared at her.

Faye swallowed. She usually had no issues with attention, but this time it was too much, especially when the reason for such rapt attention stood right behind her. Silver's presence swarmed her as if he was her shadow.

Everyone knew what they'd done, and everyone could surmise how it'd ended, since Silver was free from his chains and his eyes shone the way regular cyborg eyes did.

She cleared her throat and entered the room. "What're you doing?"

All the cyborgs were gathered around a man who was tied to a chair.

Even Edge and Heaven were there, two Fighters she wasn't too comfortable with. The way Edge looked at her, and Heaven's emotionless eyes made her feel uneasy.

Usually, Faye enjoyed men shooting her that desire-filled look that Edge gave her, but the cyborg's eyes had a coldness to them. A frigid chill that made her shiver on the inside.

The man on the chair stared ahead with an empty, but shiny gaze. His eyes shone the way Silver's had just moments ago. His dark hair hung down his shoulders and was in a desperate need of a comb.

Faye stilled. "I've seen him somewhere."

"Of course, you have," Nightmare said with a cold voice. "You saw him before I brought you to Silver a few days ago." He eyed her new cyborg, as if to make sure he was fine, but the caring glimpse in his eyes faded fast and he focused on the restrained cyborg again. "This is Sphere, if you recall. We're trying to find a way to save him."

There were other Fighters in the room, but they didn't pay much attention to what was going on. "Why in here?"

"Because the infirmary was occupied, now wasn't it?" The leader's gaze darkened, but he wore a smirk.

Faye cleared her throat and approached Celise and Wind, who also stood next to Sphere.

Silver followed her without a word.

What could he be thinking? After she'd bound him to her, she'd set him free from the chains.

Silver hadn't said anything. He hadn't even looked at her, but his resignation had been obvious as they'd cleaned themselves.

She'd wanted to say something but had been silent instead, because there were no words in the entire world that could bring him comfort.

Celise gave her a smile. "How're you feeling?"

"I'm fine."

The doctor looked at Silver. "And you? Do you want me to give you something?"

He just glared and continued with his silent-treatment.

Faye wanted to sigh but kept it in. The tension in the room said this was a bad time for her usual reactions.

She had no idea how to handle Silver, or what to do with him now. They'd agreed to stay away from each other once the bond was in place, but that was *before*.

Things were different now. He was angry, but at the same time, he stayed near her ... very near.

She studied the tied Fighter. "Have you done something to him? He isn't wild anymore."

"I've given him something to calm him," Celise answered.

Heaven and Blaze started untying the cyborg.

"What're you doing?" Faye took a step back, bumping into Silver's wide chest.

He wrapped his arms around her, tugging her closer.

She squeaked and jerked away, her heart pounding. His touch re-awakened the heat in her body. It spread around her like a warm blanket, but the last thing she needed was everyone seeing that.

Faye didn't miss the glimpse of sadness in Silver's eyes as she moved away.

"We're setting him free," Blaze answered.

She gasped. "But, he's dangerous. He was ready to jump

me when he saw me."

"The meds Celise gave him have put him at ease for a while. We need to find out why he isn't reacting to Nightmare's signal like the rest of us."

Faye studied the Fighter again.

He stood up with Blaze and Heaven on each side of him. His gaze was fixed on the floor, and he barely blinked. His head hung slightly to the side.

Celise attached cords to his head and approached a tall, slim machine next to her. There were buttons everywhere and a screen filled with text and numbers that made no sense to Faye.

The doctor pushed three buttons and returned to watching Sphere. Tension decorated her cute features.

A short silence lingered in the gathering room.

All eyes were set on the cyborg as they waited.

When Sphere finally took a deep breath, everyone seemed to relax.

He blinked, straightened his head, and looked around as his gaze focused. Confusion shone in his eyes. "What's this? What's going on?"

Celise smiled. "My name's Celise. I'm a doctor, and I'm here to help you with Blaze, Nightmare, and the others. Do you know where you are?"

The attractive cyborg frowned but then nodded. "I'm at the Fighters' Headquarters." He eyed her. "Do you work for MedAct?"

"I do, but MedAct doesn't know I'm helping you and the

other Fighters. They don't know I know about the bond."

Nightmare squeezed Sphere's arm. "You can trust her."

"We don't have much time," Celise said. "I've restored your mind, but it'll only last for a few minutes before you'll be lost to the bond's grip again. We've been trying to find a way to help you, but Nightmare's signal isn't working on you, and we can't figure out why."

"I'm not sure what's going on, but I'll answer your questions." Sphere nodded to himself, as if he was deciding to trust her after all. "I'm not sure why Nightmare's signal isn't working on me, but I have a suspicion."

"Please, tell us." Stress lingered in Celise's eyes as she glanced at the clock on the wall. "Two minutes or less left."

"My bond got damaged before my bound one died."

A loud gasp went through the room.

Faye's jaw dropped. She knew enough about cyborgs to know it was the first time anyone had ever heard *that*.

Blaze stopped in front of the Fighter, his eyes wide. "How's that possible?"

"She abandoned me."

Wind inhaled. "That's one thing a bound one is forbidden to do."

"Yes," Sphere said. "And she was punished by MedAct for it. They put her in prison, but she committed suicide a few months later. When I heard of her death, I realized what the bond really was, when it tried to kill me, and I ran. Nightmare found me and tried to help me with his signal."

Faye's heart was filled with sadness for Sphere, but also

anger for his late bound one. Every woman who signed up for a cyborg *knew* they could never abandon the cyborg.

She remembered her friend, Phoebe talking about it. The teachers at MedAct had nagged about it every day; so much that it got stuck in her head.

Faye glanced at Silver.

Their situation was different, but was she abandoning him? They'd agreed to stay away from each other once the bond was set, but Silver didn't seem too fond of the decision.

She hadn't created him. She wasn't his first bound one. She was just someone who'd kissed him to save Phoebe's cyborg, Shade from being killed. But …

She and Silver had to stay together, at least until Celise, Nightmare, and Blaze could remove the bond safely.

The last thing she wanted was Silver's death on her conscious. Sure, he was a bastard with a cocky attitude, but he didn't deserve to die, and right now, the Silver she was used to seemed far away.

They needed a clear communication to make this work, but what if they never succeeded?

He loved her but didn't seem interested in getting to know her.

Blaze placed his hand on Sphere's shoulder. "What do you want us to do?"

Determination filled the cyborg's gaze. "Don't let me die. Don't let my life be in vain."

The medic nodded. "We'll do our best."

"Find me a new bound one if you must," Sphere said.

"Just don't let me die."

Blaze stilled. "Are you sure you want that, considering what you've been through?"

He nodded sharply. "Yes. I've no idea how she succeeded with all the tests to become a bound one, but there are few like her out there. Another bound one will be nothing like her."

"As you wish."

Celise pushed a button on the machine. "Ten seconds." She glanced at Sphere. "I'll put you in a coma until we know how to help you. That way, you won't feel any more pain."

Sphere nodded. "Thank you." He smiled. There was sincerity and hope in his beautiful cyborg eyes, but a short moment later, his eyes glazed over, and his head slumped to the side.

The doctor injected something into his arm and turned to the rogue leader and medic cyborg. "He'll need an injection of this every day to stay under, but we can't keep him sedated more than just a few weeks. It will become dangerous after that."

"Let's examine his bond thoroughly first, and see if there's something you can do," Blaze told her. "If not, we'll have to find a bound one for him."

Faye moved closer. "Where are we going to that?"

Every part of her wanted to save the poor cyborg. He deserved so much better.

"That's a question for another time," Celise said. "Let's take a look at his bond first. Blaze prep the infirmary. Faye and I will get ready for the examination."

She almost jumped out of her own skin. "Me?"

Celise smiled. "You wanted to learn, didn't you?"

Everyone smiled at her.

Even Nightmare, strangely enough, but all Faye could do was stare as disbelief sang inside her.

Sure, she wanted to learn, but wasn't this a little bit overboard?

CHAPTER 11

Faye exited the infirmary unable to suppress a wide yawn. Her feet ached, her back hurt, and she could barely keep her eyes open.

This had been the most mind-blowing day of her life. First, she'd bound Silver to her, then listened to Sphere's story, and the rest of the day, she'd spent in the infirmary with Celise, Blaze, Nightmare, and Wind, trying to find what was wrong with Sphere's bond, but so far, no success.

Even Sense and Phoenix had come by from time to time.

Edge and Heaven had stayed away, even Silver, but she'd tried not to be bothered by him.

He'd stayed in the gathering room without a word.

Why? Maybe he'd had a lot to process after the bonding.

Instead, she'd focused on memorizing everything Celise had taught her. It'd been a challenge, but now, Faye's head was filled with numbers, procedures, medical terms, and anatomical differences between humans and cyborgs.

She pulled a hand through her hair and yawned again. She longed for her bed, and to rest beneath the softest sheets she'd ever slept with.

The world was wrong about the Fighters. They weren't the dirty monsters the media claimed them to be.

Everything about this place screamed cleanliness and organization with its white walls, bright lights, and lack of dust.

The sheets were her favorite thing about her sterile-looking room, and taking them home was tempting.

Nightmare knew what he wanted with this place, and the other Fighters followed without doubting or questioning him. So many were broken one way or another because of the bond, and yet, they managed to keep things together and trust each other.

The rogue leader was the first cyborg. He was the oldest, and even if Faye didn't like him much, she couldn't help but be curious about his story. She only had knowledge of the few things he'd mentioned at the abandoned house a few weeks ago.

He was one of four cyborgs who'd been created by Doctor Carolyn Williams. She'd treated them like slaves and test subjects, which had resulted with the cyborgs rebelling.

Nightmare was the only one who'd survived, and as punishment, Carolyn bound him to herself.

The leader had claimed he hadn't been bound to Carolyn until later. The bond hadn't existed when he'd been created.

A few weeks ago, a statement like that would've made her laugh.

Today, Faye didn't doubt the bastard.

She wasn't fond of him, but that was another story. He was too big, dark, and scary for her. Usually, she didn't mind a strong and cocky personality, but Nightmare was it in a serious and dangerous way that didn't appeal to her.

What had Carolyn been thinking when she'd created him? What type of woman created a cyborg like Nightmare *willingly*?

Cyborgs had never interested Faye, and she'd never taken the time to learn more about them. Now, she regretted that. Any knowledge about them and their past would've come in handy now. It would've helped her understand them— Silver—better.

Most of the Fighters seemed to like her, but at the same time, most of them held their distance. At least she'd made friends with Phoenix and Sense.

Then there was Edge.

It was obvious he didn't like her. He'd never said a single word. Instead, he always stared with an angry glare.

He was attractive, with light brown hair and masculine facial features. Short and slim for a cyborg, but he seemed fast and self-assured. And yet, there was something creepy about him, something that sent shivers down her spine.

The thought of Edge filled her with unpleasant feelings. Honestly, he was the only Fighter she stayed away from. Heaven at least didn't give her the chills the way Edge did.

She respected that the others wanted to keep their distance. Even if she was bound to Silver now, it was difficult for them to be near her. She was a woman after all.

With a deep sigh, she turned the corner.

Just a few more feet, and she'd be in her room. Even if the white and long hallways were like a labyrinth, she'd learned her way around now. She pulled the key from her pocket.

Without warning, an arm snaked around her waist.

Her scream was muffled when a masculine hand smashed against her lips.

The key fell to the floor, making a loud *clang*.

Her heart went into a frenzy when she was pressed against someone's fit chest. Whoever was holding her was strong.

Too strong for her to fight off.

"Don't move. Be silent. If you want to live, you'll do as I say." The voice was cold and filled with threatening promises.

Faye turned her head as much as she could. She had to know who was doing this. A small part of her hoped it was just a bad joke, but the firm grip around her waist and the threatening voice dashed her hope.

She bit back a second scream when recognition hit.

Edge.

He wasn't playing around. Hatred and anger radiated from his shining eyes. His grip on her face tightened.

Faye squeaked. Pain surged through her as his fingers

squeezed her jaw; she feared her bones would break. Agony made her head spin.

She grabbed his hand, desperately trying to shove it away, but Edge didn't budge.

Cyborgs were stronger than humans, but she'd never expected this.

Her eyes teared and she started to tremble. She wriggled in his arms. "Do you understand what I mean?" he hissed in her ear. "I can break you into pieces without even trying. You're like a fragile leaf in my hands, and you'll be dead long before anyone even manages to reach you."

Sweat broke out on Faye's skin and her palms were clammy. "What do you want?" Her voice quivered.

Edge jerked behind her and his head twitched to the side.

She tensed even more. She'd seen him do that from time to time. Was something wrong with his body?

Those sudden twitches could be caused by something, maybe from when his bond tried to kill him. Some cyborgs got injured when that happened. It'd happened to Sphere and Sense.

"I want you," he breathed in her ear.

She gasped when his teeth came down on her ear nib. Faye stared straight ahead as all nerve endings revolted in her entire body when he licked behind her ear.

"Walking in here was a big mistake," Edge whispered, but it had a savage bark. "Did you really believe you'd be safe here among so many broken cyborgs? It's all just an illusion. Just because you get along with a few of us doesn't mean we're nice guys." His hand trailed down her body.

She stood frozen, paralyzed from this surrealistic situation. It felt like she was dreaming, her head was heavy from lack of sleep, but she didn't move. She didn't doubt Edge would break her bones if she struggled, but on the inside, she was boiling. If she got out of this alive, she'd hit him hard where it hurt the most.

Faye clenched her fists and bit her lip.

His touch disgusted her, but thankfully, it was only on top of her clothing.

She barely dared to imagine what it would feel like against her naked skin, but apparently, that was where this was heading.

With heavy breaths, she looked around, but no one was nearby in the long hallway.

It was only them.

Her situation was hopeless.

Edge still had a harsh grip on her, and running for it would also be a mistake. She wouldn't get anywhere before he'd catch her.

Faye cursed. What was MedAct thinking, when they made the cyborgs stronger and faster than humans? They'd even created the cyborg soldiers just to protect the humans from the cyborgs. It'd ended up being a necessity.

The cyborg soldiers were the perfect military. They obeyed every order without question, but she knew even less about *them* than about the cyborgs.

Faye had seen some during her visit to MedAct, when Phoebe and Shade had been there, and they all had looked like huge and pumped bodybuilders.

She inhaled deeply when his lips pressed against her neck, and when he started showering her with kisses, she jerked away.

Edge grabbed her throat. "Don't try anything funny. I don't want to hurt you more than necessary. Don't fight me, and this will go a lot smoother."

She clenched her teeth. "You won't get away with this."

He chuckled. "As far as I know, I *am* getting away with this. Do you see anyone nearby? I don't."

She groaned when he pressed her against the wall. The impact was hard enough for her to lose her breath. She'd be badly bruised, if she managed to survive. "So, you intend to do it right here, when anyone can come by at any moment?"

"Don't worry, sweetheart. I'll be fast."

Fear filled every part of Faye's body, but so did anger. Her instincts wanted to take over. She wanted to slap him hard, but she also wanted her bones in one piece.

Somehow, she'd make him pay.

She bit her lip when he started tearing at her clothes.

He was far from gentle. Every time he grabbed her hip and face, it hurt.

Her bruises would be dark and ugly.

Edge wrapped himself around her, as if he was desperately searching for nearness. His hands went under her shirt and explored her naked skin.

His broken bond was driving him crazy, and the need for a woman was overwhelming, but what Faye couldn't understand was the hatred in his eyes.

"I thought you didn't like me." She grunted when he squeezed her breast.

"I don't. Women like *you* are the reason I even exist. It's your fault I'm in so much pain. You all deserve to suffer because of that." His hands were all over her, and when he rubbed himself against her, it was impossible to miss his arousal. "You've no idea what I go through every single day. So much pain and agony." His voice was a gravelly whisper. "Sure, Nightmare's searching for an answer to remove the bond once and for all, but it's moving so slowly forward." Edge let out a frustrated groan. "I can't take it anymore. You're my safe haven now. Since you're a bound one now, I can touch you without risking becoming bound to you."

Faye didn't say anything. She couldn't.

Ice traveled down her spine when material tore behind her. Cool air grazed her back. She cursed. The bastard had ruined her shirt. "For a split-second, you made me feel sorry for you, but not anymore. I'll make you regret this for the rest of your life," Faye hissed between her teeth, making sure he understood.

He leaned closer to her ear. "You think you can hurt me? Go ahead, try. Let's see what you've got. I don't mind a little struggle."

The sound of a zipper going down filled the hallway.

She closed her eyes when he grabbed her pants and

started unbuttoning them. Her mind searched frantically for a way out, but Faye was locked between his arms, and his strong grip held her in place.

Her body already ached all over from his rough handling, and a headache wasn't far away. Even her jaw still hurt from when he'd squeezed it.

Edge's hand trailed down her skin underneath her panties, searching for the place he wasn't allowed to touch.

She opened her mouth to scream out her fear, anger, and frustration when a loud male roar filled the hallway, echoing against the white walls.

She winced, and Edge's fit frame blocked the way for her to see anything.

He stiffened behind her, and in the next second, he was gone.

He'd been ripped away.

Faye whirled around.

Edge flew into the wall on the other side of the hallway with a loud *thump*.

Silver leaned over the other cyborg. He held Edge's shirt in his hand, glaring at the knocked down Fighter. Fury rolled off him.

Nightmare, Blaze, Wind, and Celise rushed down the hallway, all displaying various emotions.

Horror and disbelief was written over the doctor's and medic cyborg's faces, but Nightmare, and even the usually calm Wind, radiated the same anger Silver was exercising.

They all ran to her.

"Thank God," Faye mumbled and exhaled.

She was safe.

Quickly, she buttoned her pants but could do nothing about her torn shirt. Showing skin didn't usually bother her, but this time, it did. She was exposed and weak. Her hands started to tremble, and she fought the shock hitting her in waves.

She'd almost been raped.

Celise grabbed them. "Are you all right?"

Faye gave her an uncertain half-smile. Her heart thundered. "It's just stress. I'll be fine soon." She looked at Silver and Edge.

Her cyborg had both hands on Edge. He never looked her way, but his rage was unmistakable. "You son of a bitch! What do you think you're doing?"

Edge tore himself free from Silver's grip and was up on his feet within a second. He glared at everyone, then started laughing. "I'm doing what every single one of us is thinking!" The shine in his eyes intensified. "You've had your fun. Now, it's time for someone else to have fun. You don't care about her anyway."

Silver hit him with a mean right hook in the face, and a crunching sound was heard when bones broke.

It sent shivers down Faye's spine, but she was more than pleased.

Edge deserved it.

The Fighter groaned as he stumbled back but a broken nose didn't seem to bother him. Instead, he roared and lunged at her cyborg.

She gasped and jumped back to avoid getting in the way as the two Fighters went at each other.

Wind grabbed Celise and pulled her to him, wrapping his arms around his bound one as he tugged her to safety.

Faye barely noticed when Blaze grabbed her arm and dragged her away, too. She was fixed on Silver and Edge. Disbelief filled every part of her tired form.

Seeing them fight, aiming punches at each other was surreal, but at the same time, this whole situation was surreal.

She'd always known the Fighters were unpredictable because of their broken bonds, but she'd never seen *this* coming. She'd never in a million years believed one of them would try to force himself on her, and yet, Edge had tried.

Her heart refused to calm, and her hands still shook. Her chin trembled, and fatigue threatened to swallow her. It was too much, but she managed to remain on her feet.

Collapsing wasn't her thing.

Faye always somehow managed to push through. It was the stubborn side of her that ensured it.

She glanced at Nightmare as she dried away an irritating tear that'd dared to run down her cheek.

She'd expected to see anger and irritation, but what was there instead was worse.

Nothing.

Absolutely nothing.

Faye couldn't tell what he was thinking, but the

nothingness worried her more.

Other Fighters came running.

She recognized Heaven, but the other two were unfamiliar. She'd seen them, but they'd avoided her.

Faye clenched her jaw and fisted her hands when Edge hit Silver in the face. She cringed when her cyborg groaned. It was almost as if his pain was her own.

His knees gave in, but he quickly found his balance before he swung at Edge again.

Every cell in her body screamed. She had to go to him! Had to make them stop. This couldn't go on.

Faye didn't give a damn about Edge, but Silver didn't deserve this.

Why was he fighting in the first place? Was it to defend her because she was his bound one, because he loved her? Or was he just saving her from Edge because she needed rescuing?

Did she even matter beyond the feelings the bond forced upon him?

Not likely.

For some reason, that hurt like hell.

In the end, it didn't matter.

Faye had to put an end to this.

A hand landed on her shoulder when she took a step toward the fight.

She glared at Blaze.

"Don't interrupt. He's fighting for you."

Faye frowned. An uncomfortable feeling filled her.

"What do you mean?"

"What do you think it means? You're his bound one."

Silver swung his arm, hitting Edge hard in the stomach.

The Fighter let out a loud groan and went down. He landed on his ass and remained there.

His hair was a complete mess, and blood was smeared out on his face, but the hatred in his eyes remained as his snarl turned to her.

Edge breathed heavily, and his limbs trembled, but he was still strong enough to fist his hands and threaten her with his cold eyes.

Faye stood her ground, glaring right back. She wouldn't let him have the final word. She wanted his loss to sting.

Silver stood over the cyborg with death in his eyes, fisted hands, and bloody lips. He seemed just as exhausted as Edge, but he was at least standing.

Slowly, he met her gaze.

There was so much pain in his eyes, but it wasn't from physical pain, and seeing it, broke something inside Faye.

She reached for him. Her fingers trembled.

Silver winced and backed away. His gaze lingered to the floor. He took two deep but shaky breaths before he looked at her again.

Then he turned and fled.

Faye gasped and took a step in his direction.

Blaze stopped her again. "Let him go. He needs time to reflect."

She ripped her arm from his grasp. "Give me a break!"

She turned to Celise. "Do you have a scanner on you?"

The doctor blinked but reached into her coat pocket. "Here." She tossed over a small black device.

"Thanks." She was going after Silver. Determination filled every part of her. She wasn't going to let this end like this.

Then she paused. Scowled at Edge.

Heaven and another Fighter grabbed him, and pulled him up on his feet, forcing him to face her.

Faye stood in front of him, silent, just peering at him.

He didn't deserve her words. Didn't deserve her energy or time. She'd let this go and *never* think of him again.

She'd never let him get to her. The shock from his actions was slowly fading. Faye had another goal in mind, but she'd leave Edge with a gift of her own.

She swung her hand as fast as she could and slapped him hard on the cheek.

His head swung to the side, and he whined.

A stinging feeling awakened on her palm, but she didn't care. The pain was bearable, and in a way, satisfying.

Edge opened his mouth as anger radiated from his shining eyes, but Faye didn't give him the chance to say anything.

She took off after Silver.

CHAPTER 12

Silver strode away, ignoring the pain. His cheek was tender, so was his side and chest after Edge had hit him.

He'd have bruises for weeks. Hopefully, nothing was broken. It didn't feel like it, but the discomfort was more than enough.

His fists ached too, but that was an ache he welcomed. It'd felt good to hit Edge, to push him to the floor.

After what he'd been about to do to Faye, he deserved it.

He reached his room and placed his hand on the plate on the wall next to the door. It clicked, and he grabbed the door handle. Luckily, he didn't need to carry around a key as some rooms demanded.

"Silver! Wait!"

He froze.

Faye.

Silver closed his eyes and inhaled. Hearing her say his

name was like the sweetest candy. Her voice awakened all those amazing feelings, filling him with happiness, longing, and sweet thoughts.

He wanted to turn around, wrap his arms around her, and never let go.

He'd whisper words she wanted to hear, tell her how beautiful she was, and how much he longed to touch her. If he did, and she smiled at him, his life purpose would be fulfilled.

Silver cursed.

Damn bond.

She stopped behind him. "Please, wait."

He opened the door but didn't move. Faye wanted him to wait, so that was what he'd do. He had no choice but to do as she wished, at least not when it came to this.

Every cell in his body wanted to obey, but his mind knew better.

It'd almost torn him apart when she'd said they should stay away from each other once the bond was in place, but he'd somehow managed to hide it.

Silver had never agreed to it. Faye had just assumed he'd had, and he hated her for it. He hated her for what she'd done to him. Sure, he understood her reasoning, but still …

As if life wasn't tough enough.

Even if Nightmare and Celise managed to figure out how to destroy the bond, and even if they removed his bond to Faye, he'd still be in love with her.

The emotions were forced upon him because of the

bond, but once they were in place, they became *real*.

They were there to stay.

She was his everything now.

He'd die for her.

Bond, or no bond.

And Faye would never even care.

"What do you want?" It came out harsher than he'd expected, but he hadn't meant it.

Faye stopped close enough to touch him.

Her presence swept over him like a sweet caress, awakening every nerve ending in his body, creating goosebumps on his arms, and making him shiver.

Couldn't she just place her arm on him, or touch his hair, or at least do something?

The longing was slowly becoming too much. He was no longer in pain or in a desperate need to bind himself to her.

Thank God that was behind him, but now, he had to deal with these love-sick emotions instead. When he'd been bound to Claire, it'd been no issue. He'd loved every minute he'd spent with her, but now that he knew how the bond worked, he saw through it.

These amazing feelings were a curse.

Silver would never forgive Faye for this. He'd love her forever, but he'd hate her just as long. All because of one simple kiss.

Her breath shook when she inhaled. "Thank you … for saving me."

He clenched the door handle. "You're welcome." He

should turn around and hold her. He wanted to so badly, but he remained still.

Faye took a step closer. "Let me come in. I need to take a look at you."

He spun around, staring her right in the eyes. His heart pounded. Joy sang in his whole being, but he hid his smile. "You want to take care of me?"

That damn bond!

She looked him over. "You're wounded. I need to make sure you're all right."

His eyes narrowed. "Is it because you want to, or is it because you feel responsible?"

She blinked and studied him.

Was she suspecting the *wrong* answer would hurt him?

Determination filled her gaze. "Because I want to. I'm worried about you."

Pride filled Silver, and he straightened his back. This time, he was unable to hide his smug smile. "You liked what I did for you?"

"I'm … thankful you protected me from the bastard. If you hadn't shown up when you did, things would've turned ugly."

He moved closer, invading her personal space. "Yes, but did you like what I did for you?"

Faye opened her mouth, but no words came. Her chin trembled.

A pinch of anger blossomed in his heart. "It's not a difficult question."

"He had it coming, and he deserved every moment of it, but violence should never be the answer."

He snorted. "Then you shouldn't have gotten involved with the Fighters." Disappointment filled him as he turned around and entered his room. All he'd wanted to hear was a simple *"yes"*.

His room was small and simple, with white walls and a white floor. A single bed stood in one corner with a bedside table next to it. There was also a desk where he held his computer, and a wardrobe on the other side of the room.

Faye followed him and looked around. "This room looks just like mine. I guess most rooms here look the same."

The annoyance in his heart grew. "Just do what you came for and leave."

She pouted. "You don't want me here, do you?"

"You were the one who wanted us to stay away from each other once the bond was in place." Saying those words was more difficult than he'd expected, his voice had cracked a little. He hid a wince.

She cleared her throat. "Right. Remove your shirt. I'll scan you."

He obeyed without thinking. Anything to have her hands on him.

Faye studied his chest, and Silver didn't miss how her eyes widened. The silent gasp that left her lips filled him with a tiny pinch of hope.

She *did* find him attractive after all.

She took a nervous step closer and placed the cold

scanner against his chest.

He flinched but didn't move. Instead, he held his eyes on her, trying to read her.

What did she *really* want? Was there any real interest for him?

She'd said she wanted to take care of him, that she was worried about him, or had it been a lie?

He sighed.

Was he reading too much into this?

Being in love with her and hating her at the same time was a bad combination. He wanted her to get lost, but he also wanted to hold her forever.

Faye yawned, and his attention was instantly on her again.

"You're tired," he said.

She nodded as she waited for the scanner to show its results. She fixed her torn T-shirt with her free hand, but it did nothing. The material only fell back open, as it had been. "I'm exhausted. It's been a long day."

"It has." His voice was low.

Silver's blood had boiled when he'd stumbled upon Edge trying to rape Faye. He'd left after the binding to set his thoughts straight. It'd been an intense binding after all, but when he'd seen his bound one in danger, he'd completely lost it.

He'd never expected such rage coming over him. He'd never felt anything like it when he'd been bound to Claire.

Slowly, Silver raised his hand toward her face. It trembled, and hesitation ruled him.

Faye blinked and watched him with wide eyes. She didn't move, and her lips were tense.

Did she want him to touch her?

The longing and desire to do it was almost overwhelming. It could've been something beautiful. It could've been something amazing, but it was painful instead, because she didn't feel the same thing he did. She probably never would.

Once the third and final flash had happened, his feelings for her had exploded like fireworks in his chest.

Silver had gone from finding her annoying but cute to the most beautiful woman in the whole world.

There was so much he wanted to tell her, but she didn't deserve to hear it. Not yet, and maybe never.

He had no idea how things would end between them, but one thing was for sure.

There could be no happy ending.

The scanner beeped.

Resignation filled him, and Silver lowered his hand.

She blinked again and frowned.

Was that disappointment?

Faye's eyes moved as she read the information, then she relaxed. "You're fine. Nothing is broken, but you'll be bruised for sure." She removed the scanner.

"You've learned fast how to use the scanner."

She grinned. "I'm a fast learner. I understand the basics now."

He smiled back. "I would've never guessed."

She shrugged. "Just because I'm impulsive, and speak before I think, doesn't mean I'm stupid."

His gaze returned to her torn shirt. "Take it off."

She winced. "What?"

Silver pulled a T-shirt from his wardrobe and threw it her way.

Faye caught it. Disbelief shone in her eyes and she stood frozen.

He frowned.

She couldn't possibly be shy after what they'd done in the infirmary earlier.

He cursed when she didn't move and was about to turn around to give her privacy when she placed the scanner on his bed and took off the ruined shirt.

Naked and smooth skin greeted his gaze. Silver's chin dropped, and his heart skipped a beat.

She didn't have a bra on!

How hadn't he noticed that before?

Her T-shirt had been torn after all.

Damn, Faye had a body to die for, with her slim waist, wide hips, and full breasts. His palms itched for a touch, a caress. He wanted to know what they'd feel like in his big hands.

"Interested?" Her lips twitched.

She didn't even seem in a hurry to put the damn T-shirt on. She just stood there with it in her fingertips, smiling at him!

Anger surged. "Stop teasing me." His chest clenched

when she moved closer.

"Or what?"

"Or I might accept your offer." He clenched his fists.

Did she understand what she was doing to him? Did she understand how she made him feel? That she confused him?

Faye had clearly stated they should keep their distance once the bond was in place, and yet, here she was, trying to seduce him.

Everything within him screamed to give in. Silver wanted nothing more but to wrap her in his arms and kiss those sweet lips of hers. Everything about her excited him. Everything about her made him want to sacrifice his whole life for her.

He barely even knew her …

Silver cursed.

If Carolyn Williams hadn't been dead, he would've killed her! He'd never forgive that woman for coming up with something so vicious as the bond.

The temptation was almost overwhelming. He couldn't hold back, and as if in trance, he reached for her.

Faye yawned and swayed on her legs.

Silver froze.

His bound one was tired.

From one second to another, his need changed. It went from wanting to take her hard and fast against the wall to take care of her.

Her needs came first.

Always.

Right now, her need was to rest.

Silver sighed and took the shirt from her, pulling it over her head. "Arms."

Faye gave him a surprised look, but obeyed, and allowed him to put the T-shirt on her.

"You're tired. You should get some sleep." The desire in his body slowly subsided for the desire to tuck her in.

"But—"

"No buts." Silver pulled away the cover from his bed and lifted her in his arms.

She squeaked. "What're you doing?" She had no other choice but to wrap her arms around his neck.

It felt so damn good to feel her arms against him. It made him want to moan from pleasure, but he held it in. "I'm tucking you in."

"Why? I thought—"

"Because you need to sleep." Silver interrupted her again.

What she wanted to say wasn't a mystery, but her words would've hurt him more than she could ever imagine.

Seducing him and giving him her body would only work for a few moments, but deep down, a wound would open.

A wound that would never heal.

It was *her* he needed. Her presence, her understanding. Her love.

Faye wouldn't, no, couldn't give him that.

Her body came in second, and why was she offering in the first place? What could possibly be going through her mind after wanting nothing to do with him?

Silver placed her on the bed and covered her. "Now sleep."

She blinked. "I should be taking care of you, and not the other way around. You still look like a mess with blood on your face and your hair needs a brush."

He bit his lip. Hearing her say she should take care of him made him almost give in. He wanted that. Wanted to rest in her arms and enjoy the pleasure of her touch. It would calm him.

It would shut the hole in his chest.

There was nothing worse for a cyborg but a bound one who didn't fully love him. Faye didn't have any feelings for him except the feeling of responsibility, and it slowly killed him on the inside.

Silver cursed for the hundredth time. How he hated the bond!

Hopefully, Nightmare and the others would find an answer fast. He wanted nothing more but to be free from it.

At least then, he wouldn't die with Faye if something happened to her. His feelings for her would remain, but at least, he'd be safe, and it would be easier to move on.

"I'll clean up soon," he said. "Rest. You need it." He turned to leave.

Faye grabbed his arm. "Don't go."

Silver sat on the bed and held her hand. "As you wish."

She frowned.

Damn. He'd acted before thinking.

She flashed a fragile smile. "It's the bond, isn't it?"

He nodded. "Yes." He placed her hand against his cheek. Couldn't resist it anymore. He needed her nearness. "It makes me love you beyond your imagination." His voice was barely a whisper.

"But you're fighting it."

"Of course. I don't want this, and neither do you."

Faye pursed her lips, flattening the color from them.

There was something in her eyes he couldn't place. Was it sadness? Or what it just pity?

For a split-second, Silver expected her to argue about it. For some reason, he almost missed the feistiness she usually displayed, but today, she was different.

The experience with Edge had probably left a scar on her, but there was something else there as well. Something new.

Faye looked at him in a different way now. It was almost as if there was a hint of maturity there.

Somehow, he liked it.

CHAPTER 13

Silver watched Faye sleep in his bed. She'd been out in a matter of minutes. The poor thing had been completely exhausted. She held his hand in hers, and he enjoyed the heat of her skin, unable to let go.

Thousands of thoughts crossed his mind as he listened to her gentle breathing. He wanted to give in to the bond, wanted to let it take him over completely, but there was no happiness on the other side.

Faye would never welcome him into her heart.

Despite all that, he didn't want to leave, but he had to talk to Nightmare.

Silver cleaned himself up and changed clothes. It felt better to wear something fresh on after the fight with Edge.

He left his room as silently as possible to not awaken his bound one. She needed her sleep. Maybe one day he'd be allowed to sleep by her side, but he doubted. Why she'd allowed him to tuck her in was a mystery, but maybe she'd been too tired to argue.

Silver headed for the infirmary, hoping the Fighters' leader would be there. His body ached even more now than it had just after the fight. It wasn't a surprise. Although, he healed faster than a human, he still had to go through all the pain.

He opened the doors to the infirmary and scanned the area. Nightmare was there, but he wasn't alone. Celise and Wind were there. Even Heaven, Phoenix, Blaze, and Sense were gathered.

Everyone was spread out, either sitting or standing, and all their gazes landed on him as he entered.

Celise approached him, looking him over. "Are you all right?"

He snorted. The doctor in her would never let her stop. "I'm bruised, but fine."

She pulled out a syringe. "I can give you this. It'll take away the pain for a few hours."

Silver studied her, surprised she cared that much. "Aren't you afraid of me?"

Celise shook her head. "I'm not afraid of *any* of you. Everything Nightmare has shown me is true, and even if the bond is necessary for you now, I *will* help you out of it once we know how … if that's what you want."

He clenched his jaw. Was that what he wanted? He glanced at Wind before returning to her. "Is that what *you* want?"

"Wind and I have decided to not break the bond."

Wind crossed his arms over his chest. "I'm not leaving Celise. Besides, breaking the bond will probably be painful, and I've had enough of that. I will die with her when the day comes."

Silver inhaled and clenched his fists.

It'd be painful.

That much he'd figured out. The feelings were real, after all.

"No one really knows what will happen," Blaze said. "Someone will have to be the guinea pig. It might as well be painless."

Hope awakened within him. "You mean the feelings will go away?"

Hesitation lingered in the cyborg medic's red-shining eyes. "Honestly, I've no idea."

Silver sighed. No one had a clue about *anything*. "Give me the shot." He bit down when Celise injected him with the clear fluid. "Where's Edge?"

The human doctor applied a band-aid on his arm.

"He's locked up," Nightmare answered. "And he won't be coming out any time soon. I expected something like this to happen sooner or later. I just never thought Edge would be the one."

"It's not safe here for the women," Phoenix said. "Of all the Fighters, we, who are gathered here, are the most stable. The others stay away because they don't trust themselves."

"At least they're smart enough to do that," Sense said, "but

114

if Faye and Celise are to stay here, they'll need protection."

Celise looked over everyone before she spoke. "We're not staying. At least not today. We have work to do."

Silver frowned. "What're you talking about?"

Nightmare's eyes lit up and a slow grin spread across his lips. "Celise thinks we can create the first female cyborg with the program Alexander Fleming gave me many years ago. It's complete."

Silver dropped his mouth open and stared at the Fighters' leader. "Are you serious?"

"I've examined it," the doctor said, "and I think it's worth a shot. According to the information we have, the answer to the bond is in the female cyborg program. I didn't find anything that stood out, but there were indications that the answer *might* lie in its active form. If we find the answer there, we can finish Alexander Fleming's algorithm, and use it to remove the bond for good."

He swallowed, and his heart started to speed up—with hope. "You mean that she needs to be alive and active?"

Celise smiled. "It might be a hidden signal that's only visible when the female cyborg is active."

He bit his lip and tried to control his excitement. Hoping too much at this point would do him no good, but he needed to know more. "And how exactly do you plan to do this?"

"We don't have the equipment to create a cyborg, but I know where to find it."

Silver almost jumped out of his skin. "You're not making

this up, are you?" He looked around and saw echoing excitement in everybody's expressions.

The only one who wasn't showing any emotion was Heaven. The blond cyborg's emotions were shut off. They'd been damaged after his bound one had died, and he'd shut them off himself to prevent any more pain. It was all logic with him. He was here because his logic told him Celise was onto something.

Heaven's eyes betrayed nothing. They shone just like every cyborg's eyes, but they were dead, staring right in front of him, only listening to what everybody was saying.

"No, I'm not," the doctor ensured him. "I really do know where to find it, but we need to go to Glaswell first. There, we must meet up with Jade. She has the access codes we need for the facility."

"Can you tell us more about it?" Nightmare asked.

"MedAct refuses to store important equipment in the main building. It isn't one of the safest places since you try to take it down from time to time. Instead, they store everything in a facility hidden deep inside a forest about one hour from here. I've been there a few times, so I know the area."

Wind gasped, and he grabbed Celise's arm. "If you're thinking what I think you are, *don't* even think about it. You're not going." His eyes were wide, and fear lingered in them.

She appeared to squeeze his wrist. "I need to be there. Without me, the codes will be worthless. Only a MedAct

116

doctor can enter."

Silver crossed his arms. "And how exactly are you planning to smuggle us in?"

"The place is run by an Artificial Intelligence. There're no guards, and if the codes are entered, the AI will trust the doctor who enters along with her team."

He frowned, studying her. "Sounds too easy."

Nightmare moved away from the corner, approaching the doctor and her cyborg. "We'll look into every possible thing that can go wrong, but the first thing we need to do is get those codes."

Silver ran his fingers through his hair. "I guess that means I'm going to Glaswell."

He remembered a talk with his leader while he'd still been chained, and the last thing he'd wanted was to follow Faye to that forsaken place.

He'd promised himself he'd never set foot there again after Claire's death. It was a place filled with wonderful memories, but also a place filled with sorrow. He didn't want to go back.

Nightmare nodded. "You know what you have to do once you get there."

Silver nodded back. "I do, but I doubt Hunter will be interested in coming back."

"We won't know unless you'll ask."

"Hunter?" Celise asked.

"He was with us at the abandoned house when we tried to remove Shade's bond," the rogue leader said. "He got caught by MedAct, and chose to bind himself to a woman."

A deafening silence filled the room, and the sadness in Celise's eyes made him twitch.

Was she really feeling sorry for Hunter?

"Hunter deleted all his data about us," Nightmare said, "but it can be brought back if he chooses to. He was one of my best men, and he's needed if we're going to pull this off. We need an inside man. I'm hoping MedAct will accept Silver, but I have my doubts. Hunter, on the other hand—"

The doctor nodded. "I understand. Did he ... bind himself to a good woman?"

Nightmare nodded. "They knew each other from before."

"What about Shade?" Blaze asked. "Wind said he'd tell him, but to my understanding, he still doesn't know."

Silver didn't miss the uneasy gaze in his leader's eyes, and he himself, felt a sting of discomfort. Yes, Shade deserved to know, but at the same time, he could betray them all, and he wouldn't be surprised if he did.

"Let's keep him out of this," Nightmare said.

"Let's not," Celise said, and every gaze turned toward her.

"What do you mean?" Blaze asked.

"I'm Shade's doctor, as you know. Shade's bond was damaged when Nightmare tried to remove it. He's stable now, but sooner or later, the damage won't be repairable. If his bond isn't fixed, or removed, within a year or two ... he'll die."

Guilt filled Nightmare's gaze. "Does he know?"

"No. There's no reason to worry him, not yet."

"And his bound one?"

"No."

Another silence filled the room, but Silver didn't miss all the brain power working.

"Let's do this," Sense finally said. "Let's create the female cyborg."

Phoenix nodded in agreement. "There's no point to overthink things. We *need* to try."

Silver grinned as one nod after another happened. No matter what happened, this was their last chance. If they failed, there would be no more Fighters. MedAct would take care of them, and not in a good way.

There was a place where Fighters who chose not to bind themselves were brought, but they'd searched for that place for a long time to try to free the Fighters who'd ended up there.

Unfortunately, there wasn't any indication a place like that actually existed.

No name, no location.

Only a shadow and a rumor, and yet, unbound Fighters *did* disappear. They'd lost many over the years. Two had disappeared during the year he'd been with Nightmare.

Whatever MedAct did with those Fighters, Silver doubted was good, but it was a risk they were all willing to take.

It was written on all their faces. He saw it even in Celise's and Wind's eyes.

They were willing to put everything on the line for what they believed in.

Celise was a gentle person, but he didn't miss her underlying anger. Her disappointment with MedAct was obvious.

Silver straightened his back. "I'm ready for our final fight. It's all, or nothing."

One smile after another spread through the room.

They were all in.

CHAPTER 14

The drive back to Glaswell was a silent one. All she heard was the sounds the car wheels made against the pavement.

Wind drove. Celise sat next to him, and Faye and Silver were in the back.

Faye barely dared to look at her cyborg.

He'd been avoiding her since this morning. She'd awakened in his room, alone, hoping he'd return, but he never did, so she'd gone back to her room, only to find Celise there.

The doctor informed her about their plan, and an hour later, they were on their way back.

It was amazing to be going home, and a weird feeling of freedom filled her as well. She didn't need to be under the same roof as the Fighters anymore, walking around tense, never knowing what would happen.

Faye missed Sense and Phoenix. They were good buddies,

but she wouldn't miss Nightmare or Edge. She was glad the leader had taken care of Edge and wasn't going to let him roam free. After all, there was something seriously wrong with him.

It was scary to know that most of the Fighters were locked up. It showed how many of them had suffered severe damage when their bound ones had died.

She was still tense. The thought of going to her … no, *their* home alone with Silver made her shiver, but she couldn't tell if it was from pleasure or worry, but thankfully, they weren't going there first.

They'd all stop by Shade and Phoebe's place first.

"I'm not sure this is such a good idea," Faye said.

"They need to know. It's the only way," Celise said.

"I know, but I'm not sure bringing Silver there is the best thing."

Her cyborg clapped her knee. "Don't worry, sweetheart. I'll behave." He grinned but it didn't reach his anger-filled eyes.

She snorted. "Your word is just as trustworthy as the cat's promise not to chase the mouse."

His grin melded into a glare. "I would never do anything to jeopardize this."

"I don't think you would," the doctor said, "but Shade won't be happy to see you, and I don't blame him."

"Well, we can't leave Silver anywhere." Wind turned the car onto another road. "He's bound to you now, Faye. Besides, I don't think you want to leave her side. Am I right, Silver?"

Faye gazed at Silver, and when he crossed his arms and looked away like an upset child, her heart clenched.

Wind was right.

Silver *needed* to be near her, but it was because of the bond. Even if his feelings were real, she still had a hard time believing *in* them.

Sure, he'd defended her from Edge, and took care of her afterward, but he'd been cold and distant.

Was he really in love with her the way every cyborg was with his bound one?

All she saw was anger, and a glint of longing from time to time, but love? Not really.

"Shade's got time to prepare," Celise said. "I've informed him and Phoebe that Silver's coming with us."

Faye leaned closer to the doctor's seat in front of her. "How did they react when you told them about the Fighters?"

"Talking over the phone's not a good idea. I only told them we've been in contact, and that we need to talk … and that Silver's coming with us."

Faye inhaled. "I doubt that went well."

Celise cleared her throat. "I'm hoping for the best."

"Yeah, me too." She glanced at Silver again, but he was still ignoring her.

Ten minutes later, they passed through the gates to Glaswell without any issues. The guards let Silver through, too.

He was registered as hers now.

Celise had taken care of that before they'd left the Fighters headquarters. That way, he could even walk into MedAct without any consequences. He just needed to sign the contract.

He had a bound one now, after all.

It was odd, driving through the gates with him by her side. Faye had tons of questions about what would happen. This was only the beginning.

The real tests were yet to come.

Seeing Phoebe and Shade's driveaway sent chills through her, and when Wind parked the car, she held her breath for two seconds. "This is our last chance to change our minds."

Wind raised an eyebrow. "Do you really believe that's the right thing to do?"

"No."

"Then don't suggest it." He approached the door.

The insult stung, but Celise's cyborg was right. When she'd heard Shade's time was limited, her heart had almost stopped.

He was possessive of his Phoebe, and Faye liked teasing him about it, but they'd somehow managed to become friends, and the last thing she wanted was to see Phoebe devastated.

She gave Silver a dark warning look. "Behave."

He only grinned, but his irritation was difficult to miss.

Wind knocked on the door.

Faye swallowed when she spotted Shade's big dark frame blocking the entrance. The look in his shining eyes wasn't promising. It meant he'd attack if he felt threatened. Anything to protect his Phoebe, and by the look of it, not much was needed to trigger him.

Phoebe stood behind him, waiting for him to let her pass. Her cyborg was in defense mode and protecting her was his greatest priority.

"Hello, Shade." Celise smiled, but it had an obviously insecure edge.

Shade's glare didn't leave Silver. "I can't believe you brought that bastard with you."

"Nice to see you too." Silver grinned.

"I'll explain everything. Let us in and let's talk." The doctor's voice was calm.

"He's not coming in here."

Faye didn't blame her friend's cyborg.

Before Shade had had the chance to leave MedAct, Silver had shot him with a dart in an attempt to kidnap him as the Fighters had stormed MedAct's reception. Instead of taking him, they'd kidnapped Phoebe.

"You have to let him in. We can't leave him out here," Wind said.

Shade's gaze shot to Faye. "He's bound to you now?"

She nodded. "Since yesterday."

"Good. That means you can control him." He moved aside to let everyone enter.

Faye frowned to herself.

Control Silver? Was that even possible?

Phoebe smiled at everyone as they went inside, but she

shot a worried look at Silver. She studied him for seconds that felt like hours. "Don't think you're welcome here, but since Celise said she has something to tell us about you and the Fighters, I'll let you stay, but if you do anything to hurt any of us, you're out before you can even blink."

Silver raised his arms in surrender, but his grin was impossible to miss. "Don't worry, sweet Phoebe. I'm not the slightest bit interested in you. I have a bound one now." He smacked Faye's bottom.

She squeaked and glared at him.

His grin widened, but the underlying anger remained.

No one but Silver seemed amused.

Celise sighed. "Let's get this over with."

CHAPTER 15

The looks in Shade and Phoebe's eyes were exactly what Faye expected to see.

Both sat on the couch with disbelief written all over their faces. They hadn't said a word as Celise and Wind had explained the situation.

The doctor had started with what'd happened after Diane's death, and how the Fighters had come into the picture. She'd finished with showing them the information on the disc Nightmare had given her.

Phoebe gasped, staring at the holographic image of a rotating faceless female cyborg. "Is that for real? This isn't some kind of trick? There really *is* a female cyborg program?"

Celise nodded. "I've checked into it. Everything is real."

Phoebe remained still. She blinked a few times then took a deep breath and leaned back. "I can't believe this."

"Well, you'd better. We didn't go after you and Shade for

the fun of it," Silver said.

She shook her head. "I thought Nightmare and the Fighters were crazy. Everything he said sounded wrong."

"That's because you've been taught a lie from the start," Silver said. "And it doesn't help that every cyborg out there believes it, too. They don't learn the truth until they're seconds from dying, but then it's already too late. The only thing that can save them and us is that female cyborg program."

"I can confirm that," Wind said. His expression was serious. "I felt the bond change after Diane's death. I expected it to collapse and the collapse itself to kill me, but I didn't. Instead, it transformed into a poison, and there's no doubt it was designed to kill me. Without it, I would've been heartbroken by Diane's death, but I would've lived."

Shade ran a hand through his long dark curls, frustration shining through him. "You're the last one I expected to hear that from."

Wind nodded, the gravity never leaving his face. "I know. I also believed the Fighters were crazy, but after what I went through, there's no doubt in my mind the bond's designed to control us and … kill us."

Shade stood and approached the doctor's cyborg. "And that's why I believe in this, because I believe in *you*."

Wind smiled and visibly relaxed. "I figured you'd say that."

Phoebe stood as well. "Just like that?" She watched her cyborg.

Shade grabbed her hand. "I'll never forget what the Fighters did to us, but if Wind says they're right, then I believe it."

Faye smiled.

Shade and Wind had had a special relationship from the start. Shade had trusted Wind from the moment he and Diane had stepped from the elevator at MedAct. He'd instantly trusted him, and she was thankful for that.

Shade turned to Silver. His eyes were cold. "But just because I believe Wind doesn't mean any of you will be my friends."

Faye expected her cyborg to argue back, but he just studied Shade for a moment.

"You know, Nightmare tried his signal on you because he was convinced it would work. Everything pointed to it. It was based on the information Alexander Fleming gave him many years ago. He wouldn't have done it if he hadn't been sure," Silver said.

Shade snorted. "You expect me to believe that?"

"No, but it's the truth."

The air sparked with invisible arrows the two cyborgs seemed to be shooting at each other.

Faye stepped between them. "Guys, we really don't have time for this. I know you're both angry, but we need to bury those feelings if we want to succeed. Right now, we don't have much that speaks in our favor, we only have each other."

The icy sparks went on for another whole minute, until

Silver looked at *her*.

He instantly calmed, but the underlying anger still seemed to be there.

She held her breath, taking in his countenance. She felt tiny, which she physically was, compared to him, but he also made her feel insignificant on the inside.

Was she crazy for trying to control a cyborg like Silver?

Sure, he was charming and flirtatious, but he was also stubborn and impossible. He had a just as strong personality as she had, and it wasn't promising. Would that one day destroy them?

Faye opened her mouth to make them back down, but no words came. Her gaze was locked with his. She was unable to look away from his big and beautiful shining cyborg eyes. He made her pulse rise, and her heart skipped a beat. She swallowed. Hard.

She finally tore herself away, shaking her head.

What was this? Was he somehow bewitching her?

"I agree." Celise glanced at Shade. "If you and Phoebe believe what we're saying, we should move on."

Phoebe sighed and pulled her hand through her red hair. The stress was evident in her expression. "I'm not completely convinced. I'll listen to you, but I just can't see myself getting involved with the Fighters."

"You won't have to," Wind said, "but we figured you both deserve to know."

She smiled. "I appreciate that."

Wind and Celise exchanged gazes.

Faye inhaled, instantly catching up. Would they tell them that Shade didn't have long? Would they tell them that he'd die if the bond wasn't removed?

Fixing it was impossible, so the only option remaining was removing it.

Celise gave Wind an almost invisible shake with her head.

Faye relaxed. It was the right decision. Burdening Phoebe and Shade with it now would only cause them pain.

After all, the solution was still far away.

"So, what happens now?" Phoebe asked.

"We're going to create a female cyborg," Celise said. Anticipation lingered in her eyes. "For that, we need equipment. I know where it is, but to get access to it, we need codes only Jade has."

Phoebe bit her lip. "That won't be easy."

"No, but we have a plan. Before we left the Fighters' headquarters, I registered Silver as Faye's cyborg, meaning, in MedAct's eyes, he's no longer considered one of the Fighters. He can walk around without any issues now, but Jade still needs to come by and make him sign a contract."

Phoebe frowned. "I'm starting to see where this is going. Jade will have to come here, and while she's busy with Silver, you'll hack her computer and steal the codes."

Wind smiled. "Exactly."

"I'll book a meeting with her once we're done here," Celise said.

"Do you need us to be there?"

Celise nodded. "It would help. The more to distract her, the better."

Phoebe sighed. "Fine." She shoved her fingers through her hair again. "I can't believe I'm doing this." She sat on the edge of her couch. "I've seen all the evidence, and I've heard Wind's story, but it's still hard to comprehend." Disbelief colored her features.

"You just need time," Faye said.

Silence filled the room as Phoebe seemed to struggle with the whole situation. One second, she looked confused, wearing a frown, and in the next, she seemed relaxed, as if she'd slowly started to accept everything, only to go back the disbelief.

Faye glanced at Silver. In a way, that was what she felt when it came to the handsome blond cyborg. She both wanted and didn't want him in her life. But she still didn't know which side was winning.

CHAPTER 16

With a lump in her throat, Faye opened the door to her home. Silver's presence lingered over her like a shadow as he followed her inside. The world suddenly felt a lot smaller as the thick panel closed behind him.

Alone.

They were *alone* in her little house, and her heart pounded like never before. Before they'd left Phoebe and Shade's, Celise had asked if she wanted to sleep over at her and Wind's instead, just in case.

No one trusted Silver yet, and neither did she, but spending the night somewhere else wouldn't make things better between them. She doubted he'd appreciate it, and in a way, she wanted to show him that she *wanted* to trust him.

He was her cyborg, after all, and bound to her.

The realization slapped her in the face.

What in the world should she do with him?

133

"Well, welcome home, I guess." She threw out with her arms and swallowed when she met his gaze.

Silver didn't seem impressed. "*This* is where you live? It's tiny." He looked around in the living room, which was connected with the kitchen.

On the other side of the room was a door, leading to the bedroom, bathroom, and wardrobe. The living room contained a couch, a television, a table, and a bookshelf. Two huge landscape paintings decorated the walls.

Faye frowned. "I don't need much. Do you really think I want to clean and wash my life away?"

His lips twitched, but the anger she'd seen in him the whole day didn't subside. "I guess not."

She turned toward the blue couch and put her bag on it. "We're not moving."

He frowned too. "I didn't ask."

"No, but you were thinking it."

Silver took a step closer. "So, you read minds now?"

"Don't be stupid. Of course, I don't."

He flinched, and for a split-second, hurt masked his handsome, masculine features.

The change in the air was instant. It became heavy as a brick and almost impossible to breathe.

Had she said something wrong? Had he flinched because she'd called him stupid?

"Whatever," he muttered and headed for the bedroom.

Faye followed and watched him place his heavy bag on the floor, clearly stating he was moving in.

Silver threw himself on the bed with a satisfied groan and placed his arms behind his head. The content grin was impossible to miss. The hurt seemed to be washed away.

The bed was king-sized, and yet, when he spread out, it looked small. He filled it with his six-foot-three frame, and biceps bigger than her thighs. She barely dared to compare his long legs to any part of her body.

She crossed her arms over her breasts and glared. "What're you doing?" Trying to sound irritated failed when her voice trembled.

Silver propped himself on his elbows. "What does it look like? It's getting late, and we should get ready for sleep. I'm exhausted."

Her chin dropped. "I'm not sleeping with you! There's a perfectly fine couch in the living room, and you can use it."

He frowned. "Do you expect me to sleep on the couch for the rest of your life?"

Faye held her breath. He hadn't said *his* life. He'd said *her* life. That was like another reality slap right in the face.

He didn't expect to survive her death.

They really needed to get rid of the damn bond as soon as possible. The last thing she wanted was him dying with her when the day came.

"I won't apologize for kissing you. I won't apologize for binding you to me. You had it coming for what you and the others did to Shade, but you already know that. That being said, you know where we stand. The bond is temporary. As soon as Nightmare and Celise figure it out, you'll be free.

135

We'd agreed to keep this relationship on a friendly level, but we're barely that. You don't want to get any closer to me than I want to get closer to you."

The silence that filled the room was deafening, and the way Silver glared at her amazed her that her heart was still beating. His dark look alone could kill her in a second.

Instinctively, she took a step back.

"You're forgetting, my feelings for you are here to stay."

She'd never heard his voice that cold before.

"What did you think would happen when you kissed me? I doubt you even thought it through."

Faye stood her ground. She wouldn't allow him to scare her. "No, I didn't think it through. All I wanted was for you and the others to stop beating Shade, and apparently, it worked. Besides, I didn't even believe you could get bound to me from one simple kiss. It sounded too weird."

"And yet, here I am."

"Yes, and I still think you should sleep on the couch."

Silver flew up from the bed in a millisecond.

She squeaked and before she could process it, he had her pressed against the wall, locked in between his strong arms.

The sound from when he slammed his fists against the wall echoed in her head.

Anger radiated from his shining cyborg eyes.

Maybe she should've listened to Celise, after all. A sleepover didn't sound so bad right now. She held her back straight even if every part of her body wanted to curl up. "Don't you dare hurt me."

"I can never hurt you. It's impossible. You're my everything, whether I want you to be, or not. Without you, I'm dead. Literally."

"You'll live a long life once the bond's removed." She licked her lips.

Silver slammed his hand into the wall again and roared out in pure fury. "Do you even have the *slightest* idea what you're doing to me right now?" He grabbed her shoulders and squeezed, but not hard enough to cause her pain.

Then he leaned closer.

His warm breath grazed her face, and Faye shivered.

A gentle gasp left her mouth when he placed his cheek against hers. She felt his desperation in that tiny action, and even if she wanted to ignore it, she couldn't.

He loved her.

Whether he wanted to or not.

Was he even able to keep this relationship on a friendly level? Did he want to?

Her hands trembled when she reached for him. Faye hesitated for two long seconds before she placed them on his broad back and slowly stroked him.

Slowly, Silver started to calm, and let out a deep exhale.

Her heart tripped, increasing her breathing as their gazes locked together.

Whomever Claire, his late bound one, had been, she'd created a magnificent cyborg. It was hard to not look at him and admire his masculine handsome features.

His blond hair hung down his shoulders, and no matter

how the wind messed it around, it still looked good. It'd only been that one time, when he'd been chained to the wall, that he'd looked like a complete train-wreck.

"Tell me," she asked with a low voice. "Tell me what I'm doing to you. Help me understand you better."

"You know how the bond works."

She nodded. "I do, but I don't know how it makes you *feel.*"

Silver remained silent, just studying her. He didn't push her hands away either. Instead, he allowed her to keep caressing him. There was something in his eyes that told her he desperately needed to be touched.

After a long silence, he sighed and rested his head against her shoulder.

Faye froze. Having him this close, having his body against hers with the wall at her back, made her feel tiny once more.

His strength was even evident from the gentle feeling of his head on her shoulder.

"Why do you want to know?" he asked.

"I told you the day I came to set the bond. I want to get to know you."

He snorted. "You're not the slightest interested in me. All you care about is the removal of the bond. That's all you ever talk about. I'm not even allowed to sleep by your side. You want us to stay away from each other." The coldness in his voice started to return.

Faye felt his muscles tense. "That's what you want as well."

"I never said that."

"But—"

Silver slammed his hand against the wall again, making her jump. "No buts. I never said that, and I never will. I hate you for what you did to me. I hate you for taking away my freedom. I'll never forgive you for kissing me and making me want you, but I never wanted us to stay away from each other once the bond was set. To me, that's suicide."

Confusion sang inside her. Her hands sank to her sides. "I ... I don't understand. You always made me believe you don't want anything to do with me."

He grabbed her wrist and lifted it. He pinned her arm against the wall. "I don't want anything to do with you, but my love for you burns stronger. You have me wrapped around your little finger, and I want to be your happy little puppy." He pulled back and looked her deep in the eyes. "I want to give in."

She was unable to move. Even if she noticed pain in every word he uttered, she couldn't get away from how he affected her.

He made her body come alive. His words ignited every nerve ending of her lower parts, making her sex clench, and butterflies awaken in her stomach.

Faye wanted him to give in. She wanted to find out what it would be like to be completely and fully loved by someone.

She'd had a few relationships over the years, but none of them had worked out, and none of them had ever been like the love a cyborg could give her.

That complete devotion.

She'd never had that with a human man, but she'd never wanted a cyborg either.

The responsibility and determination had scared her. She'd learned it was impossible to grow tired of your cyborg, and yet, Sphere's bound one had abandoned him.

Everything was so different now.

One part of her wanted to hug Silver. That part wanted to hold on to him and never let go. She couldn't deny the attraction she felt for him.

For some reason, he always made her heart flutter, but would she ever feel more? Would she ever be able to become a true bound one? A bound one a cyborg—*her* cyborg— deserved?

Faye couldn't stop her gaze from lowering to his lips. Neither could she stop herself from tilting her head and lean closer.

Whatever drove her, she had no control. It was a need she had to fulfill. A need that was caused by a mix of emotions.

It was everything from sadness and pity, to desire and want. Her loneliness surfaced. Being alone for several years had been starting to get to her, but she wasn't alone anymore.

Silver was here, and he could become everything she ever wanted him to be.

She pressed her lips against his, feeling the heat from his. She didn't miss his nearly-silent gasp, nor the gentle wince or the tension of his muscles. Faye liked the way he pressed himself closer to deepen the kiss.

She liked the way she affected him.

Silver tugged his head away, interrupting the kiss. He panted, and the anger returned. "What're you doing?" The coldness in his voice was back.

She frowned. Her lips felt empty, missing his. "I'm kissing you."

His eyes narrowed. "Why?"

Faye winced and opened her mouth to speak, but no words came out. What did she say to that?

"If a friendly relationship is what you want, then that's what we'll have, no matter how much it hurts me," he hissed between his teeth. "But don't ever play with me. Don't ever. Play. With. Me." He slammed his fist against the wall a third time before he stormed out of the room.

She heard the front door open, and then slam shut.

The house suddenly felt so big …

… and quiet.

CHAPTER 17

Fury rippled through Silver's veins as he stalked down the sidewalk. He needed to get away from Faye even if his bond wanted him to go back. It made him want to hold her, to breathe in her scent, and never let go. But *he* wanted to just get away.

This entire situation drove him crazy. It was obvious she didn't have any interest in him.

He was only a responsibility, and damn, that hurt.

He'd been furious from the moment she'd kissed him in that abandoned house. At first, Silver hadn't understood what'd happened, but then he'd felt the bond come alive.

The bond had taken over, and his only thought had been to go to her, to finish the binding, but Nightmare and the other Fighters had stopped him. They'd dragged him out from the place.

He barely remembered how he'd gotten back to the

Fighters headquarters, and the following days had been a mess as well. All he remembered was pain, and that fierce tormenting need to seal the bond.

It'd felt like an eternity before Faye finally showed up to seal the bond, and here he was now.

Deeply in love.

Hating every minute of it.

There was only one way for him to go. He had to accept the bond and the love for her. Struggling against the bond would only make his life more complicated, and he had enough pain as it was.

The knowledge she'd never love him back broke his heart into pieces.

Silver cursed.

She just *had* to kiss him.

Even if Nightmare and Celise would be able to remove the bond, his love would never go away. That was the only part that was real. The bond wasn't designed to remove the love. Why should it, when it was designed to kill him the moment his bound one died?

Silver closed his eyes and paused.

An image of a smiling Claire popped up in his head.

His beautiful Claire, with long blonde hair and big green eyes. Her mesmerizing smile had always made his heart pound harder, and he'd spent hours just devouring her beauty. That had been enough to make his day.

How naïve he'd been back then.

At the same time, not knowing the bond's real function

had been a sweet oblivion.

He'd been happy, really happy.

Now, all he had was pain.

Silver sighed.

There really was only one way out of this, and that was accepting the bond.

For now …

He remained still, and calmness slowly swept over him.

The bond liked his way of thinking. It wanted to be accepted. It wanted him to go back to Faye and hold her, but he wasn't ready to do that.

Was he even ready to give in to the bond?

It was the right way, the *only* way, because who knew if Nightmare and Celise would ever figure out how to remove the bond. In a worst-case scenario, he was stuck with Faye for life.

He shivered. Being stuck with a woman that would never love him was a complete nightmare. How on earth would he be able to live like that?

Silver opened his eyes, staring out in front of him.

Could he make Faye fall in love with him?

Did he even want to?

"Silver?"

He turned when he heard someone say his name and met the surprised gaze of Hunter.

The dark-haired and tall cyborg stared with wide eyes and a slack jaw, but then he relaxed and smiled. "I guess the woman that kissed you got her hands on you." He reached for his hand. "I thought I'd never see any of you again."

Silver's lips twitched as they shook hands.

If Hunter only knew.

"You won't get rid of us that easily."

The other cyborg frowned. "Us? You're still one of the Fighters?"

"I'm a bound cyborg, accepted by MedAct. Meaning, I'm a good boy now." His grin widened.

Hunter snorted. "You mean, you're a wolf in sheep disguise."

Silver chuckled. "You know me so well."

His old friend shook his head but kept smiling. "I know you, and I know Nightmare, but all my information about the Fighters is gone. I deleted it to keep you guys safe. Did you do the same?"

"No, and I won't. A lot of things have happened since you left. I planned to call you later tonight."

Hunter studied him with a frown.

Silver didn't blame him for being suspicious. Every Fighter had vowed to delete that fragile information if they were ever caught by MedAct.

"Let me guess," Hunter said. "Nightmare wants me back."

Silver nodded. "You're needed. Tomorrow, me, my bound one, and a few others are meeting Jade Silva. She's going to do her basic stuff, but the real point with the meeting is to steal codes from her computer."

He had no issues telling Hunter the truth. The cyborg

was trustworthy. He'd been one of Nightmare's best men, and he still was, with or without the information about the Fighters.

"What codes?"

"They'll help us get into a place where we're going to steal some equipment."

Hunter blinked. "What for?"

He beamed. "We're going to create a female cyborg."

Silence filled the street, only the wind was heard. For a long moment, neither of them spoke and Silver didn't rush. Hunter needed time to process what he'd just said.

Then the cyborg gasped. "You've found the answer?"

"Not yet, but we're getting there."

Hunter took a step closer. His eyes were wide with curiosity. "Tell me."

"I will, but not here. Is there a place we can talk?"

He nodded. "Mine and Avril's house is just around the corner. We can talk there."

Silver hesitated. "Is your bound one home?"

"Yes, but don't worry. She knows everything."

He gaped. Hadn't expected that. "You told her?"

"Of course. We spent a few days at MedAct after the bond had been sealed. We'd thought Jade would keep us there for weeks, but she let us go after less than a week. Since I'm a previous Fighter, she helped us get a house inside the walls of Glaswell. Not everyone is fond of previous Fighters, but in here, we're safe."

Silver nodded. He'd never seen it happen, but he'd heard

stories about previous Fighters who'd gone back to living a regular cyborg life. Humans didn't trust them and had in groups attacked some of them. It hadn't ended well.

"I've known Avril since she was a child," Hunter went on, "so don't worry. She's trustworthy."

Silver frowned. "And did she believe you?"

He shrugged. "She does believe me but isn't really sure what to think. She doubts the Fighters would go through all that for nothing, though."

"Just as I thought. I guess that means you must bring her tomorrow to Shade's house. We'll be meeting there. Your bound one will find the proof she seeks there."

Hunter studied again, silent. "Things have really changed since I left, haven't they?"

He could only laugh. "You've no idea. You're in for a surprise, but for that, we need to activate your memories."

A spark of hope awakened in his old friend's eyes. "Nightmare gave you the activation codes?"

Silver snorted. "You think I'd seek you out without having the codes with me? Who do you take me for?" He gave a wicked grin.

Hunter smiled again. "Even if it has been a few weeks, it feels like forever. I've missed you guys."

"You're missed, too. Nightmare nagged me about bringing you back almost every day."

He frowned. "Really?" Suspicion sounded in his voice.

"Well, he told me to bring you back … twice."

Hunter burst out laughing. "I figured. Being spoken

about twice by Nightmare means I'm very important."

"Something like that. Lead the way to your house. We have a lot to talk about."

CHAPTER 18

Silver opened the door to Faye's house as quietly as possible. It would take some time before he saw this place as home. It was dark outside, almost one a.m., and she was probably asleep.

Guilt swept over him for leaving her alone for this long, but he'd needed it.

He'd needed to breathe.

Meeting Hunter had helped him think of other things. They'd spent hours talking with his friend's bound one. He'd decided to trust Avril, even if he'd been cautious in the beginning.

She was a stranger, and strangers usually didn't think highly about the Fighters, but Avril had a Fighter bound to her, and that eased Silver's suspicion.

It didn't take much convincing for Avril to accept the situation, and now, he was here, back inside Faye's house.

Hunter's memories were restored, and he and Avril would meet everyone tomorrow at Shade and Phoebe's house. Silver had informed everyone over the phone before leaving Hunter and Avril's.

He took off his shoes to avoid making noise. If Faye was asleep, he didn't want to wake her, but he doubted she was.

Apart from a small light coming from the bedroom, everything else was dark in the house.

Silver approached the bedroom. What should he say if she wasn't asleep? Would she even look him in the eyes?

After how he'd treated her before running away, it wouldn't surprise him if she didn't want anything to do with him.

That hurt.

That actually really hurt.

He took a deep breath, preparing for a confrontation, just in case, and entered the bedroom.

Silver froze, and his heart almost stopped.

Faye lay on her side on the bed, hugging a pillow. She was asleep, but the pillow was wet.

Wet from her tears.

The sight almost killed him on the inside and he no longer could fight the bond. It swept around him like a glove, awakening the great need to protect her from harm. Even from himself. It was overwhelming, and tears ran down his cheeks.

Silver closed his eyes, fisted his hands …

… and gave in, surrendering to the bond.

His love for Faye exploded in his heart, sweeping over him like a warm blanket.

Now that there wasn't any resistance left in him, it took completely over, filling him with all the amazing emotions he'd tried to push away.

His heart broke when he saw what he'd done to her.

He'd made her cry.

Silver would never do that again.

Instead, he'd hold her in his arms, wrap her in his love, and protect her from harm. Even from himself. He'd be the cyborg she deserved to have.

He'd always be by her side and make her happy.

He'd even die for her.

Who would've believed he'd ever reach this point? He'd expected a lifelong fight against the bond, but no more. He couldn't handle it anymore, and she was too beautiful ...

There was only one thing to do.

Dry her tears forever.

Without a second thought, Silver removed his clothes but left his underwear on. He turned off the light and lay down next to her, wrapping her in his arms.

The feeling of her head against his chest and her body against his made him tingle all over.

A calmness filled him, and it was the best emotion ever.

He was *home*.

Faye stirred from all the movement and looked up with glazed sleepiness. Her eyes widened when she met his gaze. She gasped and tried to push him away. "What're you doing?"

Silver tightened his grip. "I'm holding you."

She pushed harder. "Let me go." Anger radiated in her voice.

"Never."

She stilled, staring at him with obvious surprise. "What?"

"I've given in. The bond rules me, and I'm on a new mission now."

"What?" she said again, her surprise even greater.

Silver moved on top of her before she had the chance to react.

A squeak left Faye's mouth, and it was impossible to miss the hint of fear that filled her. Then the anger rose to new levels. She pressed her nails into his skin, banged on his shoulders, and pulled his hair. "Get off me!"

He sighed, grabbed her arms, and pressed them against the bed. Her attempt to get away barely budged him.

She glared, pulling at her arms without success. "You're so going to regret this."

He frowned. "Please, tell me. I'm so curious about how exactly."

"I'll forbid you to ever see me again," she hissed.

The hurt sang in his heart. "I guess *you* would do a thing like that." Silver placed his mouth near her ear. "But do you really think I'd let you go? Have you already forgotten what I just told you?"

She swallowed. "You said you've given in."

Silver pressed his cheek against hers. Being this close to her was the most amazing feeling ever. The heat from her body wrapped around him, and he enjoyed every second of it.

Her feistiness didn't bother him. Instead, he found it amusing and cute. Despite her size, she had more spunk than most. The only way for her to get away was if he pulled back, and yet, she kept wiggling, wringing her arms, constantly attempting to get free.

"Yes, I've given in. Do you understand what that means?"

She stilled and remained silent for a mere second. "You've accepted me as your bound one."

"Exactly, and that means I want nothing more but to make you happy." He kissed her cheek, gently brushing his lips on her skin, and earning a gasp in reward. "I don't care if you want a cold relationship. I don't care that you think it would be best if we stayed away from each other. I only care about making you see how much you need me." He raised his head and looked her in the eyes.

Faye's were wide, shock evident in them, and her chin trembled. She wasn't struggling anymore. "You're crazy."

Her words stung his heart again. "No, not crazy. In love. I'm in love with *you*."

Her chin trembled even more. "You don't really want this."

"No, I don't, but there's no way out, not now, not ever. The last thing I want is to be miserable for the rest of my life, so I decided to accept the bond." Silver chuckled. "You've got no idea how good it feels right now. I've forgotten how amazing it was to be in love, to feel like this for another. It tickles all over, and all I want to do is please you." He turned serious. "But you don't want any of it. Therefore, I have a mission now."

Worry filled her gaze. "You mentioned that."

He grinned. "Do you know what it is?"

Faye frowned. "How the heck do you expect me to know?"

He let go of one of her wrists, giving her the chance to get away, but she didn't move. He didn't miss the glimpse of curiosity in her eyes.

Silver slid his fingertips down her arm, awakening goosebumps all over her skin. Even if her words denied him, her actions and the obvious desire spoke another story.

That was the story he intended to awaken.

"I'm going to make you fall in love with me."

CHAPTER 19

Faye couldn't believe her ears. This huge brute who just recently fought with all his might *not* to be bonded to her was now telling her he'd accepted the bond and intended to make her love him.

She would've laughed if it hadn't been for that serious look in his eyes.

Mixed emotions lingered in her heart. A few days ago, she'd been sure about what she wanted, but she had no idea what she wanted now.

It mostly felt like a defense-speech every time she told him she wanted things to remain on a friendly level.

A part of her liked being pinned down. Faye even wanted to part her legs and see where it would lead. He'd felt so damn good inside her when they'd sealed the bond.

Was it possible for her to love him?

Sure, she found him attractive and, in a way, she also

enjoyed his annoying personality, but love was far-fetched.

Just because she wanted him didn't mean she'd ever fall in love.

"And how exactly do you intend to do that?" she asked.

The shine in his eyes intensified. "I'll start with showing you how good we can be together."

Faye snorted. "We're the perfect miss-match. We're both stubborn enough to piss each other off for a lifetime or two."

"I'll prove you wrong."

Disbelief filled her. Had he really switched over? Just like that? "I don't believe you. Where does all of this come from? Just a few days ago, you didn't want anything to do with me."

"It's been on my mind for a while. You've no idea how emotionally painful it is to go against the bond. It's unpleasant to a level I started to feel sick. I struggled hard after you kissed me, but the bond wanted nothing more but to be sealed. It almost drove me crazy."

She swallowed and almost drowned in his deep and longing-filled eyes. It awakened butterflies in her stomach.

That deep and shining gaze lingered on her face. He looked at her as if there was nothing more exciting to look at *but* her.

Silver almost made her feel important.

Faye's heart clenched. "You're not angry about me kissing you anymore?"

"What's done is done. I can only move on, and that's what I'm doing. I'm accepting the situation, and so should you. Maybe Nightmare and the others will one day find the answer. Maybe the female cyborg *is* the answer." He went silent for a moment. "Or maybe she's not."

"You're hoping, aren't you?"

"No, I'm not. It's pointless. My feelings for you will remain whether the bond's removed or not."

Her tummy trembled.

Why didn't she, all of a sudden, like the idea of removing the bond?

"You want nothing more but to remove it." He leaned down, almost touching his lips to hers. "I'll make you change your mind. I'll make you miss me, and I'll make you see you need me. When I'm done, you'll want nothing more but to be by my side for the rest of your life."

Damn, her heart was acting up a lot today. It was cantering, and her lower part clenched with desire from his words.

Silver awakened a need she'd never felt before. No man had ever had such effect on her.

"It can save your life."

He touched his cheek to hers again. "It can, but I've had enough pain for a lifetime." With one swift move, he parted her legs and pressed himself against her.

Faye gasped from the sudden move, but it was impossible to miss what part of him was there, and it felt really good.

Silver nipped her ear. "I'm going to make you want me so bad, you won't be able to stand to be without me."

The tingling feeling in her stomach grew as his warm

breath caressed her cheek. Anticipation lingered in every part of her body, and she couldn't wait to see what he'd do next. The excitement was almost overwhelming. She longed to have her arms and legs wrapped around him as he thrust hard inside her. The image made her sex clench.

She could barely wait.

His passion was unmistakable, and there was no doubt she'd soon be in heaven.

The longing grew rapidly in her gut, and if he hadn't been holding her hands pressed to the bed, she'd caress him all over, but Silver wasn't moving.

"What you're waiting for? Go ahead." She gave him a wicked grin.

He remained still, just watching her. Then, he lay down next to her.

Faye blinked. "What're you doing?"

He wore a calm expression. The desire was still there, but it was slowly dying and was replaced by a gentleness she'd never seen before.

Where had the charming and cocky cyborg gone?

"You'll give your body to me without a second thought because you want me, but it's not your body I'm trying to win. It's your heart," Silver said.

She flew up. "You son of a bitch! You started this, and now you're going to leave me hanging?"

He grabbed her arm and pulled her down on her back, wrapping his arms around her. "No, I'm not. I'm going to take good care of you, but we won't have sex again until your heart belongs to me."

Faye stared at the ceiling as disbelief filled her, but she didn't struggle against his embrace. After all, she liked being held by him.

His sudden change was a huge surprise. Probably the greatest shock of her life. Silver placed his head against her throat, snuggling against her. His big strong hand started slowly to caress her, awakening goosebumps all over her body.

Who'd believe this strong smart-ass cyborg had such gentleness within him?

She didn't move. She had no idea what to do. One part wanted to yell and tell him a thing or two about their relationship, but the other part slowly started to comprehend he wasn't playing.

Silver really meant every word he'd said.

He'd given in to the bond, and he was going to do everything in his power to make her fall in love with him.

A pinch of excitement filled her. Faye looked forward to it; couldn't help it. "Do you think I'll fall in love with you just because you're caressing me?"

"It's one tactic, and it's working."

She flinched. "What makes you say that?"

He grinned. "Because you're not trying to get away."

Her cheeks burned. "Well ... who doesn't like to be caressed? It's nice, and it doesn't have to mean anything."

"You can't lie to me." Silver raised his head and his fingers touched her cheek, awakening even more goosebumps on her skin. "I can see it in your eyes."

Was she that easy to read? "See what?" She wasn't going to give up that easily. Wasn't going to make this simple for him.

The deep, and somewhat, smug look he gave her made Faye hold her breath. The heat in her belly refused to die.

Having him this near and looking at her with those marvelous shining eyes of his didn't help.

Silver was, without a doubt, a great seducer. She didn't question that. She'd seen it firsthand, and he was about to use every trick in the book.

How on earth was she supposed to fight a thing like that?

"I see your interest," he whispered. "You want this."

Well, damn. She really was like an open book.

"You still refuse to see the attraction between us. You still push me aside and imagine you want things innocent, even if you know that will never work. Not between a cyborg and a human. My bond will never accept it."

She pushed her chin up. "So, what're you going to do? To change my mind?"

"This." With one swift move, Silver grabbed her arms, placed them above her head, and pressed his lips against hers.

A squeak left her mouth.

He was excellent at surprising her today, and at first, she had no idea what to do. After just a short moment, she was kissing him back.

Faye had kissed guys before, but none of them had

awakened cozy and sweet emotions within her. He made her come alive. It sent her head spinning and made her world blossom.

She didn't even mind the idea of falling in love with him anymore.

Maybe being with Silver wouldn't be so bad, especially if he was going to be like this from now on.

She liked this.

She liked it more than she'd ever expected.

CHAPTER 20

Faye knocked on the door to Shade and Phoebe's home.

Silver stood next to her, holding her hand.

Since that morning, he'd barely left her side. He watched her like a hawk, and now, when they were about to enter a house filled with people, he looked tense.

Everyone would be there. Shade and Phoebe, Wind and Celise, and Hunter, with his bound one Avril.

"Ow," Faye growled and snapped her hand free from his grip. "You're squeezing my hand."

Silver winced. "Sorry. Didn't mean to hurt you."

She frowned.

He was apologizing? That was new.

The door opened, and a smiling Phoebe gave her a big hug. "Finally. We've been waiting for you. Everyone's here but Jade."

Faye tensed. If everyone was already here, it meant

Hunter and his bound one was as well. She hadn't seen him since the abandoned house, where Nightmare had tried to remove Shade's bond to Phoebe. She barely remembered him, but Shade, without a doubt, did.

"Don't worry," Phoebe said, as if she read her mind. "Shade and Hunter have already spoken. Everything's fine."

She nodded. "Good." Silver didn't leave her side.

It was starting to get on her nerves. Was he going to stay attached to her during their entire visit?

She glared. "What's wrong with you?"

He opened his mouth to answer but didn't get the chance to speak, because the hallway got filled with people.

Faye squeaked when she saw Celise and wrapped her into a big hug. "How are things going here?" she whispered in the woman's ear. "Any explosions yet?"

Celise chuckled. "It was tense at first, but Hunter and Shade quickly came to an agreement. Besides, his bound one is really nice."

Faye looked over the doctor's shoulder and met Hunter's gaze.

He smiled, but she didn't smile back.

A dark-haired, beautiful woman stood next to him. She barely reached his shoulders, but the way she grabbed his hand with a soft and caring caress revealed she was his bound one.

Faye moved toward them.

Silver grabbed her arm and pulled her back.

Surprise filled her. "What're you doing? I was about to say hello."

"You can do it from here. You don't need to approach them." He squeezed her arm again, like he'd done before they'd entered the house.

She frowned. "Excuse me?"

Hunter chuckled. "The need to protect you from everything and everyone is overwhelming him. I guess he has accepted the bond."

Faye didn't like the understanding look everyone gave her. She wanted to explode and tell her cyborg a thing or two, but when she noticed the pinch of despair in his pretty eyes, she stilled.

His gaze spoke words he hadn't said aloud. The cheeky and flirtatious Silver wasn't there anymore. Instead, she met the eyes of a cyborg who was ready to die for her.

He pulled her against him, glaring at everyone. "Don't come any closer. I'm hanging on a thin thread."

Learning to trust Silver had been a challenge. She still didn't trust him wholly, but when it came to defending her, she believed him. He *would* attack anyone who came too close.

"We'll just say hello from here," Hunter's bound one said, and waved. "Hello, Faye. I'm Avril." She smiled.

Faye grinned. "Nice to meet you, I guess."

"Don't worry. We've been informed about everything and we'll help."

She nodded, but could they trust them?

Faye glanced at Celise and Wind. "So, what's the plan?"

Hunter answered instead. "I'm going to hack Jade's

computer while she writes the contract with Silver."

Faye's eyes narrowed. She didn't like that one bit. "Why you?"

"Because I'm the most capable cyborg. I was Nightmare's hacker. Jade's aware of our capabilities; therefore, her software is well-protected, but she's not aware of the extent of my knowledge." He grinned.

She rolled her eyes, but when Silver pressed her harder against him, he made her gasp.

"Don't talk to her!" Silver's voice boomed through the hallway.

Hunter raised his hands and took a step back. "All right, I won't. I guess no cyborg should speak to her today."

"That would be wise," her cyborg growled.

Faye frowned. He was taking this too far. "How on earth do you expect that to work? Do you expect me to ignore their existence for the rest of my life?"

Phoebe moved closer. "His possessiveness will calm down, just play along for now. We all want to remain in one piece."

She let out a frustrated puff. "Unbelievable."

"Am I interrupting something?"

A new voice filled the hallway.

Jade Silva stood in the doorway wearing a serious expression. Her strong gaze lingered on everyone for a short second, and it sent shivers down Faye's back.

Despite her attractive appearance and short figure, the CEO of MedAct was not a woman to take lightly. She

165

radiated confidence, and a *"don't-you-dare-question-me"* attitude.

Her dark brown hair was put in a ponytail. She wore tight jeans and a regular T-shirt. No doctor's coat, like Faye was used to seeing her in.

Jade was not alone.

Behind her stood a massive cyborg, and a gasp went through the room when everyone noticed him.

He literally was a giant. There was no better way to describe him. He was handsome, with masculine features and blond hair, but even though his eyes radiated kindness, and a pinch of sternness, everyone in the hallway took a step back.

A cyborg soldier.

Crap.

Faye hadn't expected the doctor to bring a cyborg soldier with her, and apparently, neither had anyone else.

"What's Soul doing here?" A frown was written on Celise's face.

Faye didn't miss the pinch of worry in her friend's expression. Did she worry their plan would fail?

This cyborg could ruin everything.

Jade entered the house, and the cyborg soldier followed. "He's here for my safety. You didn't expect me to come alone, did you?" Her gaze locked with Silver's and Hunter's.

How Jade had known Hunter would be here too, Faye didn't know. Maybe Celise had told her the day before.

Phoebe made a move toward them, wearing a stiff smile.

"Well, you're both welcome to our home. We thought it would be more fun if we all gathered here now that Silver is finally with us." Faye's best friend looked at the cyborg soldier and put her hand out. Her fingers trembled. "I'm Phoebe."

The cyborg soldier shook her hand and flashed a gentle smile. "I'm Soul."

The last thing Faye had expected to see in the eyes of a cyborg soldier was gentleness. She'd heard how fierce and deadly they were, and despite his size, he reminded more of a big teddy bear right now.

"You're bound to Jade?" Phoebe asked.

He shook his head, and his lips turned slim as his gaze hardened.

Where did the pinch of dislike come from all of a sudden?

"My bound one's at MedAct right now. She's one of the doctors who work there," Soul said.

No one seemed to have missed his sudden change, but no one seemed eager to ask him more either, even if the questions obviously lingered in their minds.

Faye crossed her arms over her chest. Well, she'd change that fast. "What's her name?"

"Janice Walker."

"And she just lets you walls out with another woman?"

Soul's lips twitched. "We're not like regular cyborgs."

"What exactly does *that* mean?"

Silver pulled her closer, if that was even possible, but he didn't say anything.

Strange.

He'd been ready to attack Hunter for just talking to her, but when it came to *this* cyborg, he didn't say a word.

She gave him a quick look and froze.

Fear.

Fear was written in his shining eyes. He was trying to hide it, but it shone through.

That didn't make sense. Why did he, all of a sudden, fear a cyborg soldier?

Faye didn't remember seeing any fear in him when he'd been captured by MedAct not so long ago.

"It means, I do what my bound one orders me to," Soul answered with a straight face.

There it was again. The dislike. It appeared just as fast as it disappeared.

"Really? You'll do *anything* she says?" Faye asked.

He lips turned white and a long silence filled the hallway.

This awkward conversation awakened her curiosity.

There was more to this cyborg soldier than she'd imagined. He honestly didn't seem too fond of his bound one, and that was unheard of.

Cyborgs always fancied and adored their bound one, so why didn't Soul? What had he been through?

Faye glanced at Celise and could tell she was thinking the same thing.

They had to find out more about this. Maybe there was something they could use against MedAct.

Jade headed for the guest room. "Let's do what we came

here for, shall we?"

"Of course," Celise said, and followed.

Wind was right behind her.

Faye entered the living room slowly, keeping a watchful eye on the cyborg soldier, just like everybody else seemed to be doing. She chose to stand instead of sitting, just in case. Sitting could be a disadvantage if something happened.

Jade placed her bag on the couch and looked at Silver. She studied him under a long and unpleasant silence.

Faye didn't like the way the doctor looked at her cyborg. The suspicion, she didn't blame, but did she have to look so angry?

What ever had Silver done to her?

Faye clenched her knuckles, ready to defend Silver if needed.

She winced.

Wait, where had *that* come from?

"So, tell me," the head doctor began. "How did the two of you find each other? According to what I know, the Fighters dragged Silver away from the abandoned house before I and other doctors arrived to save Shade from Nightmare."

That wasn't difficult to answer. Before leaving the Fighters headquarters, they'd all agreed to a story that Jade would easily buy.

"He sought me out," Faye said.

Silver nodded, still clinging to her side. "The Fighters kept me imprisoned for a while. They worried I'd hurt Faye, but the need to bond with her took over, and I escaped."

"And how did you find her?" Jade's voice was filled with that same suspicion.

"I assumed she lived in Glaswell, so I started looking here. I also scanned a few computers once I came close enough to someone's home and found her address."

The doctor turned to Faye. "And what did you do when he showed up?"

"I freaked out, of course. I never expected him to appear on my doorstep. The following days were turbulent, but to make a long story short, I bound him to me, and here we are."

Silver placed his arms on Faye's shoulders and grinned. "One small happy family."

Jade kept studying them. "I assume you both agree to the contract?"

"Yes," she said. "I'm taking my responsibility. At first, I thought he deserved to suffer for what he and the other Fighters did to Shade, but when I saw how much pain he actually was in, I decided to bind him to me." Faye looked at Silver, giving him a loving smile.

Strangely enough, acting the smile was easier than she'd expected. It felt almost natural. She caressed his cheek without giving it a second thought.

Silver's gaze shot to her and a spark of love awakened in his eyes. He looked at her lips, and she understood where his thoughts were heading. He wanted all this to be over so that they could go home, but when she remembered what he'd said yesterday, her heart skipped.

He was going to make her fall in love with him.

Silver wouldn't touch her before she *was* in love with him.

Jade's lips twitched. "How cute." Her smile faded and she grabbed a laptop from her bag.

Faye tensed. That was the laptop Hunter was going to try to hack. If the codes weren't there, he'd connect with MedAct through the laptop and hack the doctor's main computer at her office. As long as she used the same password, it shouldn't be an issue.

If not, they were screwed.

Hunter sat on the couch opposite the one Jade sat on, with Avril by his side. There was a seriousness in his eyes, and his gaze was focused on Jade's laptop. He tilted his head slightly when the doctor started it, and his focus intensified.

Faye gazed at everyone in the room.

Wind sat on an armchair with Celise on his lap.

Phoebe sat on a chair and Shade stood behind her with his hands on her shoulders. Everyone looked just as tense as she felt.

Not good.

If they didn't relax soon, Jade would suspect that something was going on. Or worse.

Soul would suspect.

She burst into a fake smile and approached the set table. Everything from tea and coffee to delicious desserts and cookies stood there. "How about something sweet, everyone? It will break up all this tension. Let's remember, we're all friends." Faye took a plate and put a cookie on it, handing it to Jade.

The doctor took the plate. "Thank you." She ate the cookie as she pushed some buttons on the keyboard.

Faye relaxed. Good. She wasn't suspecting anything, and everyone else seemed to take a collective breath as well.

"Good idea," Phoebe said and approached the table. "Let's eat and talk."

Soon, everyone had something yummy to feast on, and a warm drink to wash it down with.

The mood instantly improved.

Jade looked at Faye and Silver. "Are you two ready to sign the contract?"

"Yes," he answered for both of them.

"Good. I see that Celise has already registered you in our system as Faye's cyborg, meaning, Celise's now your doctor, and you're no longer considered a Fighter. Do you understand that?"

Silver's gaze darkened. "Don't tell me what I am. You don't decide that."

The head doctor of MedAct frowned. "No, I don't, but you can't contact them again."

"And what will you do if I do? Threaten me? Or worse! Remove me from your cyborg system?"

Jade didn't look impressed by Silver's attitude. "You won't be given a second chance. You'll be directly sent to XenthAid."

Everyone's interest suddenly pitched, and a loud gasp

172

went through the room.

"XenthAid?" Phoebe wondered aloud.

Jade's eyes widened as she stared at everyone for a long second, then sighed. Resignation filled her. "That's classified information. You were not supposed to know that."

Silver grinned. "Well, now that you've said A, you must say B."

She clenched her fists. "XenthAid is where we send cyborgs who aren't able to function in society. They can never leave, but they get good lives."

"We've all heard of a place like that," Wind said, "but there's never been any evidence of it ever existing."

"Like I said. It's classified information. Not even I know where it is."

Silver snorted. "You expect me to believe that? You're the CEO of MedAct! You *should* know!"

"I'm just one person, and *MedAct* is my responsibility, not XenthAid. I, and the CEO of XenthAid, communicate regularly. She writes me monthly reports, shows me pictures of what's going on, and more." Her voice turned hard. "XenthAid is a safe place. Stop being such a bastard."

Silver looked like he wanted to explode.

Faye grabbed him by the arms. "Relax. I'm your bound one, and you'll do as I say. Let's get this contract-thing over with."

He shot her a surprised look. "Do as you say?"

"Yes, now shut up."

Jade chuckled. "Yes, shut up, and let's sign the contract. I

173

have other things to do." She pushed a button on the laptop, then she pushed it again, harder. "What's wrong with this laptop today? It's been messing with me ever since I opened it."

Faye swallowed a breath. She wanted to look at Hunter, but one simple glimpse could awaken suspicion. Instead, she pretended to be bored and rolled her eyes.

"Let me take a look," Soul said.

The doctor handed it over.

The tension instantly shot up in the room.

She didn't need to look at her friends to see it, to know what everyone was thinking. What if Soul discovered Hunter's interference?

Who knew what he'd do then. Would Shade, Silver, and Wind even stand a chance against him?

The silence was defining as Soul examined the laptop.

Faye dared to glance at Hunter. She needed to know what was going on, if they were safe or not. She should be able to see it on his face. Her heart pounded as their gazes met, but thankfully, the hacker cyborg seemed calm.

He wasn't even paying any attention to what Soul was doing. Instead, he pulled Avril to him and kissed her forehead. He asked her something, but Faye didn't hear what.

Avril gave him a sweet smile and said something back.

Hunter nodded, and they chuckled together.

Faye's chest tightened. They looked happy. She knew nothing about them, nothing more than that Avril had bound a Fighter to her, and they'd known each other in the past. Avril's love seemed deep. She'd wanted more than just to save a Fighter from certain death.

Her love was true and pure.

Envy filled Faye. She could have that with Silver … if she wanted.

All she had to do was stop fighting.

"Done," Soul said and handed Jade the laptop. "A virus tried to make a mess. I stopped it. Everything should be fine now."

Jade's gaze darkened. "A virus? Why didn't the anti-virus program stop it?"

"It did, but the virus avoided it somehow."

Shit.

Not good.

Was the soldier cyborg onto them?

The way he looked around at everyone wasn't promising.

The CEO sighed. "Let's get this done." She pushed a few keys on the laptop, then gave it to Faye. "Everything we say now will be recorded. It will be your contract with MedAct. Please place your hand on the screen."

Faye obeyed with a pounding heart, staring at the blue screen as it blinked a few times under her palm.

Silver was officially becoming hers.

It was a weird feeling.

Jade stood and stared her straight in the eyes. "I, Doctor Jade Silva, hereby open the contract with Faye Summers regarding the cyborg, Silver, who was created and awakened by MedAct. He's been a Fighter for almost a year but was kissed by Faye some time ago, and they have now agreed to sign a contract." She took a short pause. "There's no way out of this contract. Only death can release you from it. Mistreating Silver in any way is punishable, and you'll be supervised the first two years by doctor Celise Campbell. Do you understand?"

Yikes. That sounded way too serious, but she could only nod. "Yes, I, Faye Summers agree."

"Good. Give the laptop to Silver."

Her cyborg took it and placed his hand on the screen. The light showed up and scanned his hand.

"Do you, Silver, a former Fighter, agree to be bound to Faye Summers and to abide by MedAct's laws?" Jade asked.

His gaze darkened, and he opened his mouth to speak.

Faye grabbed his arm. "Don't say anything stupid."

He sighed. "Fine." He looked at MedAct's CEO. "I'll follow your stupid laws."

She snorted and took the laptop from him. "I figured you wouldn't be pleased, but the contract is now set. You're officially bound to Faye."

"That's the only good thing that has come from all this." He grabbed Faye and leaned in for a kiss, his gaze sparkled with amusement.

She squeaked and pushed against his chest. "What the heck do you think you're doing?"

"Kissing you, of course. We need to celebrate." He leaned in for a second attempt.

Faye smacked his cheek. "Give me a break!"

Laughter came from all the corners of the room, even Jade seemed amused. "Well, good luck with your bound one, Silver. You're going to need it."

Faye's cheeks overheated. He was making her blush like a teenage girl, and the way he grinned at Jaye, with promise written all over his face, didn't make it any better, but she couldn't get away from the feeling that one part of her *liked* this.

"She'll love me in a matter of days," Silver told Jade. "You just wait and see."

The doctor packed her bag and threw it over her shoulder. "Like I said, good luck. The rest is up to the both of you." She turned to Phoebe and Shade. "Thank you for the hospitality." She headed toward the front door, and Soul followed.

Silence filled the living room once the door closed behind them.

No one moved.

No one dared to speak, as the sounds of Jade's car disappeared in the distance.

Faye couldn't believe they'd gotten to this point, but the question was; had they succeeded?

Everyone's head turned to Hunter.

"Did you get it?" Celise asked.

The tension in the air was so thick it was almost impossible to not hear everyone's heart pounding.

A wide grin split Hunter's face. "I got it."

CHAPTER 21

"Didn't that go a little bit too easy?" A frown decorated Nightmare's dark looks.

"It did," Celise said. "That's why we don't have much time. We must do this as soon as possible. We won't get another chance."

They were all in the gathering room in the Fighters' headquarters. Every Fighter that wasn't locked up was there, listening and planning.

Faye had never felt more cramped.

Even if the room was huge, there were almost thirty people there. Some stood, some sat on the couches, and others leaned against the wall.

Every single Fighter had a serious expression written all over their faces.

Not just that. Although she was a bound one now, and the Fighters bonds didn't count her as a potential bound one anymore, she still didn't feel completely safe.

One of them could snap any minute, just like Edge had. Luckily, he wasn't here today, but who knew what went through their heads. Their bonds screamed inside them, after all. Despite their devotion to the cause, their pain was impossible to miss.

They were the Fighters.

The dangerous and unpredictable cyborgs the world didn't want anything to do with.

Neither Hunter, Avril, Shade, or Phoebe were present, and Faye didn't blame them. Hunter was bound now, and Shade didn't want anything to do with the Fighters more than necessary.

Celise and Wind were there, and they stood near Blaze and Nightmare. The doctor seemed oblivious to the potential danger with so many Fighters around. She was too swept up in the planning.

This was a critical moment.

They had to get everything just right, or they'd fail, and they'd never get the chance again. They needed the equipment to create a female cyborg. Without it, there was no way for them to move forward.

"When?" Silver asked. He stood behind Faye with his hands on her shoulders.

His touch made her feel safer.

Her big blond cyborg would protect her if something happened.

"Tomorrow", Nightmare said.

"I agree," Celise said. "Hunter said that Jade, or someone else, *will*, sooner or later, discover her laptop has been tampered with. I wouldn't be surprised if Soul suspected it when he checked it."

"True," Blaze said, "but will they know what we were looking for?"

"They'll realize it eventually, therefore, we don't have much time."

The blond Fighter, Heaven, moved closer. "I'll prepare the vans. How many are going?"

Faye didn't know what to think of the attractive and muscular cyborg Heaven.

He barely spoke or involved himself in any of the conversations. He stayed in the background. Heaven only opened his mouth when it was necessary, and when he did, it sounded stiff, almost robotic, in one voice tone.

His eyes were dead, as if they were drained of all emotions. There simply wasn't anything there. Apparently, Heaven had turned off his feelings after his bound one had died. Somehow, that had saved his life.

"I'm going," Nightmare said. "We need at least two vans. We'll be getting a lot of equipment."

"And that's why I'm also going," Celise said.

Faye gasped. "What?"

The doctor spared her a glance. "I have to. I'm the only one who knows what we need."

Wind didn't look the slightest bit excited. He stood with tense lips and fisted hands but didn't say anything.

Obviously, he agreed they needed her help.

"You can't be serious," Faye told Celise. "It's dangerous."

"I know, but do you have a better idea?"

She gaped, unable to find an answer. She shot a look at Wind. "Aren't you going to say something?"

The cyborg gave her a sad smile. "Celise and I have already talked about it, and even if I don't like it, she's right. We can't forget one single thing. If we do, it can ruin everything, but don't worry, I'm not letting her go alone."

Faye sighed. "You're both out of your minds." She placed her hands on her hips. "Fine, I'm going too."

Silver spun her toward him. His eyes were big, filled with fear again.

Then it hit her.

The fear she'd seen in his eyes when he'd spotted Soul entering Shade and Phoebe's house. He hadn't been afraid of the cyborg soldier.

He'd been afraid *for* her.

A lump got stuck in her throat.

"You're not going!" her cyborg hissed. "I'm not letting you get near that place."

She took a deep breath, ready to argue, ready to yell and state her point over and over again, but when she looked into his shining eyes and saw the desperation, her fire died. Instead, she grabbed Silver's hands. "I'm going, big boy, and nothing you say, or do, will stop me." She kept her voice calm, almost soothing, and it seemed to work.

He stared, insecurity lingering in his expression. He seemed to be fighting with himself. He remained silent for several moments, switching from one emotion to another. Going from anger to frustration, to desperation and sadness.

Then he took a deep breath, straightened his back, and all emotions washed off him. Silver looked at Nightmare. "I'm going."

Faye snorted. She wasn't a bit surprised.

Celise shook her head. "Faye, I really think you should stay."

She frowned. "Do I need to tell you what I just told Silver, minus the *'big boy'* thing? You can't change my mind. Besides, you're going to need me."

"Why?"

"For moral support, and for carrying the light stuff, of course."

The doctor's lips twitched. "Fine, but if anything happens to you, I'll never forgive you."

Faye grinned. "The same applies to you."

"Deal."

Blaze rose from his chair. "I'll stay here and prepare the infirmary, just in case. We never know what might happen. I'll be on standby, along with a few other Fighters." He looked around, locking gaze with three other cyborgs.

Faye didn't know their names, but they each gave a nod. Maybe, they also had some medical skills.

"I'll drive the other van," Phoenix said and grinned at her. "I'm a mean driver."

Sense, who stood next to her friend, chuckled and smacked his arm. "You sure are. I have to find new wheels way too often because of you."

Phoenix shrugged. "At least, I'm having fun, something all of us need more of."

Sense nodded. "True." He looked at Nightmare. "Count me in."

A few more volunteered, and five minutes later, they had a full team, ready to go.

She licked her lips. She doubted anyone had ever tried breaking into wherever they were going. "Where exactly is this place?" Faye asked Celise.

"About an hour away, in the middle of a forest. There're no guards, only an Artificial Intelligence. With the help of the codes we took from Jade a MedAct doctor can enter. That's why I need to be there." She gave Wind a look.

He didn't say a thing, but his lips were a flat line.

Celise pulled out a big paper from her bag. She placed it on a table and everyone gathered around it. "I prepared this before leaving home. It's a map of the area. As you can see, a high stone wall surrounds it, and there's only one way out. We'll need a man there, keeping an eye on unwanted guests."

A brown-haired cyborg raised his hand. "I can do that."

She nodded. "There's only one huge warehouse on the inside. It's a labyrinth in there, but we only need to focus on the shelves closest to the gate, and the storage room."

"Good," Nightmare said. "That'll make it easier." He stood with his arms crossed over his chest and deep focus in his shining eyes. He was cataloging every single word Celise said.

Faye grinned.

183

The world feared him. He was considered the most dangerous, unpredictable, and fierce Fighter out there. The crazy look in his eyes and the dark vibes he radiated didn't ease that impression.

The news gladly scared every child, woman, and man with Nightmare's actions. They showed him storming and raving buildings, taking out police cars, and blowing up things. No wonder people feared him.

Yet, Celise had him wrapped around her little finger.

"I'll open the warehouse with the codes we got from Jade. Once on the inside, we'll need to grab everything fast." The doctor whirled the map around, showing a big interior image of the warehouse. "This is what it looks like on the inside, roughly speaking. I had to draw everything from memory, but I doubt anything has changed." She pointed to each area. "Everyone who's going inside will get a task, and you'll do nothing else but pick up the things you've been assigned to find. If someone lags behind, you only help once your own mission is completed. Understood?" She looked at everyone, getting nods back from every direction.

Faye grinned. "I really like your new attitude. Where did all that strength come from?"

Celise's cheeks turned red. "I'm just passionate about this."

Nightmare chuckled. "She'd make a perfect leader."

Wind's gaze hardened. "Keep dreaming."

The doctor cleared her throat. "Moving on. The most difficult thing will be the tank. We must plan that one out thoroughly. It should also be our main goal. Without it, we have nothing. With it, I can improvise."

"You should be assigned to the tank," Blaze told her.

She winced. "Why? I can't help lift it."

"No, but it's our most precious gem, is it not? If something goes wrong, we're toast."

Celise nodded and her chest heaved. "True."

"Tell me about the tank," Heaven demanded.

"It's huge and heavy, made from glass and metal. It's about eighth feet, so we'll need a big van to transport it."

"We have several vans, and I know the perfect one for this mission."

She smiled. "There're several tanks stored there. Before we grab one, I'll need to check it to make sure it's functioning. Once that's done, it will be easy to move. They're all stored on wheels. You guys will only have to lift it into the van."

Phoenix pouted, disbelief filling his expression. "This sounds so simple."

"If everyone knows their role, it *will* be, but we need to keep our eyes open. Who knows if Soul and Jade have figured out that her laptop was messed with or not."

"They'll come for us," Nightmare said, his voice darkened. "They always do."

"Then let's make sure we're ready for them", Faye said.

Nightmare locked gazes with her. His serious expression melted into a grin.

She grinned back.

Maybe he was starting to trust her.

CHAPTER 22

"This has to be the longest hour of my life," Faye said and sighed.

She sat in the back of the van, and Heaven was driving. The vehicle was white and clean on the inside, just like everything else that had to do with the Fighters headquarters.

The van was filled with everything they could possibly need. Flashlights, ropes, tools, and more, and the equipment was neatly stored in metal boxes that were attached to the floor.

"We're almost there," Celise said.

"I don't like this," Wind said and clenched his fists.

"Who does?" Silver grumbled from his seat next to Faye.

They'd barely said anything during the long ride to the warehouse where their future awaited.

Either everything would be fine, and they'd get their hands on the tank and all the equipment they needed, or this was the last day of their lives.

"I was looking forward to growing old," Faye quipped.

No one filled the ensuing silence. They all seemed to have disappeared into their own heads.

For a long while, the only sound was the wheels rolling fast on the pavement.

It was night outside, pitch dark. They were all dressed in black, equipped with weapons and night vision glasses.

Faye felt her gun against her leg where it was hanging. Before leaving, Silver and Nightmare had taught her, Wind, and Celise how to shoot, just in case.

A few hours of practice didn't make her a professional, but at least now she wouldn't risk shooting anyone by mistake.

The plan was simple.

Get in, get what they came for, and leave.

Everyone knew where they were supposed to go, and they were all divided into groups of at least two. No one would be alone, and no one would play a hero.

She couldn't recall how many times Nightmare had shouted that into everyone's heads, and thankfully everyone took him seriously.

This wasn't a game.

Their future depended on this.

Nightmare sat next to Wind, his gaze focused on the floor.

Faye didn't have to guess what was going through his mind. He'd been waiting for this day for over forty years.

He'd been searching for an answer for so long but never gotten anywhere, then Celise had come into his life, and everything had changed.

Not just for him, but for all the Fighters.

If someone would have told her a year ago she'd join them, she would've laughed. Yet, here she was, out on a crazy mission only God knew how it would end.

Worst-case scenario, MedAct, and their cyborg soldiers were already waiting for them.

Phoenix was driving the other van, and it was ahead of them. It was a lot bigger, and the tank should fit, according to their calculations.

Sense and other Fighters were in that van as well. Their mission was to take care of the tank. Plenty of hands were going to be needed. Some Fighters had guard duty, to make sure no one snuck up on any of them.

"We're here," Heaven said from the driver's seat. "I can see the gate on the GPS."

Everyone was instantly wide-awake.

Faye's heart tripped over itself.

This was it.

"Slow down," Nightmare told Heaven. "We need to be sure no surprises await us up ahead." He lifted the radio to his mouth. "You heard me, Phoenix?"

"I did," the cyborg answered on the other side of the line. "Slowing down."

A short silence followed. Faye couldn't see anything because she was in the back, but this was the moment of truth.

If someone stood by the entrance gate, the plan was to continue driving and go for plan B. Climbing over the wall was not a possibility, since barbed wires covered the top. Plan B was simple. Wait further down until the coast was clear.

"We're good to go," Phoenix exclaimed through the radio.

A big collective exhale went through the van.

"We're going to phase two," Nightmare said. "Get ready."

Faye sat tense, staring at the floor. She had nothing to do with phase two, but Celise did.

As soon as the van stopped, the rogue leader opened the doors. He, Wind, and Silver jumped out with their guns high, all scanning the area.

Another silence followed.

"It's clear," Wind said.

Celise jumped out.

It was time to open the gate.

Faye closed her eyes. She wasn't religious, but she prayed now. It'd be a disaster if the codes turned out to be wrong.

The doctor had to do a lot of things to be allowed to enter. Not only did she have to program in the codes they'd stolen from Jade, she also had to scan her palm, eye, and enter her own code before the I.A would let her in.

They could all only hope the CEO hadn't become suspicious and removed Celise from the list of the MedAct doctors who could enter this facility.

One minute after another seemed to pass, and the

tension in Faye's body grew.

This wasn't a good sign.

"Come on, Celise," she mumbled.

Movement from the opening of the van and crackling sounds from outside made her look up.

A smiling Celise entered, followed by the Fighters. "It's done. The gate is opening."

"Oh, thank God." She felt herself relax, but this was just the beginning. At least they were in. "Was it difficult?"

"No. Everything worked as it should."

Faye smiled. "That's promising. Maybe Jade didn't suspect anything, and all this will work out just fine. Maybe we worry in vain."

"Don't let your guard down." The Fighters' leader's serious gaze made him look dangerous, deadly. His black long hair, the scar on his throat, and his powerful radiance screamed it. Right now, he really was the cyborg most people feared.

Faye didn't let that scare her. "I don't intend to."

Silver grabbed her hand, and her attention shot to him.

He'd been by her side since he'd given in to the bond. It'd been three days since that night.

She'd never seen the change coming, and hadn't expected what she'd gotten.

Her cyborg had spoiled her rotten with breakfast in bed, massages, beautiful words, and amazing embraces. He barely left her side, and all these wonderful things were slowly growing on her.

Silver had still kept his word. As long as she wasn't in love with him, they wouldn't have sex, but he held her tight throughout the night, and his warm and strong body started to make her feel safe.

Faye even missed him those short moments when he was away to talk to Nightmare, or just going to the bathroom.

The leader closed the back doors, and as they drove through the gate, Silver pulled her close, wrapping his arm around her.

A week ago, she would've hit him on the head for doing that. Today, she leaned into his embrace. Closed her eyes, enjoying the silent minute it took to get to the warehouse.

For the first time in her life, Faye felt safe in a way she'd never felt before. She was starting to trust every word that came out of Silver's mouth. Sure, he was still cocky, and flirtatious, but whenever he spoke about his emotions for her, he was always serious.

The past three days had been amazing.

He snuggled his face against her throat, inhaling her scent and his arms tightened around her waist. "I'm not going to let anything happen to you," he whispered in her ear.

Her lips twitched. In a way, it was cute, this over-protective thing he was doing every day, and hopefully, it wouldn't get too annoying in the future. "I thought you'd stop me."

"That was the idea, but I realized it was a pointless battle."

"I would've come along anyway, no matter what you said."

Silver chucked. "I know. The only way to stop you would be to lock you up."

She tensed. "You thought about doing that?"

"Yes, but my mission is to make you love me, not hate me, remember?"

Her grin returned. "And how's that coming for you?"

He let out a satisfied sound, as if he'd just eaten something tasty and sweet. "You like me, even if you're not willing to admit it yet, but don't worry. I'm far from done trying."

A tingling sensation awakened in her gut. One part of Faye looked forward to his attempts. She couldn't wait to find out what else he'd do to win her over. The excitement made her forget how their relationship had started. Besides, getting away was futile. He was bound to her now.

He was hers.

Silver would even die for her.

He'd follow her anywhere she ran, but running was the last thing on her mind.

She chuckled and shook her head.

Silver raised his head. "What's so funny?"

"You know, I never imagined this," she whispered, "but I really like where we're heading. You're not as annoying as you used to be."

He flashed a wide smile filled with pride. "See? You'll be head over heels in love with me in no time."

Faye snorted. "In your dreams, big boy." Trying to sound

serious was difficult. She was unable to hide her enthusiasm and smile.

Silver chuckled and kissed her cheek. "You're such a bad liar."

Faye had to agree. She couldn't put words to what she felt for him, but she couldn't deny the attraction.

He pulled her in like a flower was pulled to the sun. She'd drown in his amazing shining eyes if it was possible. Her arms felt empty without him.

This was evolving into something she'd never seen coming, and in a way, she liked it. She didn't want to fight it, not anymore.

He'd given in.

Maybe she should, too.

"We're here," Celise said when the van stopped.

"Get ready," Nightmare ordered.

The back doors opened. Heaven stood there with a huge gun in his hands. He looked frightening, with his black clothes and emotionless eyes.

Faye spotted the other van from her seat.

Phoenix, Sense, and the other Fighters exited it, raised their weapons and started spreading around.

Heaven joined them.

"Stay here until the warehouse is open," the leader told Faye, and looked at Celise. "Let's go."

The doctor tensed but left the van with Wind by her side.

She took a shaky breath and grabbed Silver's hand. "Are you ready?"

"As ready as I can be."

Their mission was simple. While Celise and the others took care of the tank and other necessary equipment, her and Silver's task was to gather medicine.

All they had to do was run through the warehouse and head for the storage. The doctor had drawn them a map that Silver had memorized, and as soon as the door to the warehouse was open, their task was on.

Faye shook her limbs out. "We can do this."

Her cyborg grabbed her face and pressed his lips to hers.

She winced from the unexpected kiss, but gave in when she felt his passion and despair in every caress with his tongue. She allowed herself to drown in his embrace.

Who knew, maybe it was the last one.

Silver looked her deep in the eyes. The fear in them was evident. "Don't ever leave my side."

Faye swallowed. Nerves started to get the better of her but seeing his was almost too much. She didn't want him to be in pain. "I won't."

Maybe coming here hadn't been one of her brightest ideas. She'd only thought of herself, eager to enter another adventure, but now when they were there, all she felt was the reality of the situation.

Hopefully, nothing bad would happen, but if Soul and Jade had figured out what they'd done, they were doomed.

MedAct's cyborg soldiers would be almost impossible to defeat.

Silver could get hurt.

That worried her more than she'd imagined.

What if *she* got hurt?

Silver would die if she died.

A lump got stuck in her throat, and she wrapped her arms around him and showered him with kisses.

Silver chuckled. "You've never kissed me like this before." A glint awakened in his eyes. "I like it."

Faye didn't smile back. "Don't die on me."

Surprise filled his expression. "So, you do care."

She stilled, his words hitting her like a slap in the face. The truth fell out. "Yeah, I do."

They shared a look, an expression that said more than words ever could.

Faye saw the love he felt for her. There was no doubt, Silver had really given in to the bond.

Until now, a small part of her had questioned it, even if he'd been completely different these past few days, but now, she *knew*.

Now, she was sure.

Nightmare showed up. His expression hard and stern, filled with determination. "It's time."

CHAPTER 23

Faye ran through the warehouse, following Silver. It was massive and mazelike, filled with goods stacked on high pallet racks or shelves. Luckily, they knew exactly where they were heading. It'd been enough for Silver to see Celise's map once. Cyborgs had an amazing memory.

"We only have five minutes," she reminded him when he slowed to look around another corner.

"We won't have five minutes if we can't reach the room alive."

True, but he was being too cautious. The warehouse seemed empty.

As soon as they'd entered it, they'd started looking around, searching for an ambush, but nothing.

"I'm not going to die." Faye hoped that was enough to get him going.

"No, you're not, because I'm going to protect you. I'll be

your armor."

She bit her lip. Silver *would* take a bullet for her, and that was the weirdest feeling ever. She had a hard time getting used to the idea that he'd die for her, but that was the bond's curse. A cyborg would always choose to sacrifice himself instead of his bound one, and she hated it. She didn't want him to die because of her, but one day, he would, whether she wanted it or not.

Silver held a steady grip on her hand. He wasn't squeezing too hard, but hard enough to not lose her.

His strong and warm hand was a safety Faye desperately needed. Her heart galloped from all the stress, but her focus was on the mission.

They had to succeed.

She had no idea how Celise planned to create the female cyborg since her friend lacked the education, but with Blaze's help, they'd be able to figure it out, Faye hoped.

"We're here," Silver said, and they stopped in front of a closed door. On the wall next to it was a digital plate. He entered a code, and there was a *click*. She entered and scanned the place. The room wasn't big, but well-lit and filled with cabinets loaded with all types of medicine and medical equipment.

Faye recalled what Celise had said and located a cabinet with the number *342* written on it. She had no idea what the number stood for, but it didn't matter. They were supposed to empty it and return to the van.

"There," Silver said and approached the huge white

cabinet as he unzipped the bag they'd brought with them.

Faye opened the cabinet. "Wow. There's a lot here. Thankfully, nothing is glass. At least, we won't have to worry about glass splinters in the bag if something breaks."

They worked in silence as fast as they could. Faye had no idea what any of them were for, but Celise had explained some were needed to create the female cyborg. The rest was to help the Fighters, to ease their pain.

She studied her cyborg.

Silver moved with ease, but the way his muscles worked, and the way his hands tensed around each bottle made her lick her lips.

Each finger was a piece of art along with the strong veins on the back of his hand, creating a masterpiece. It made her mind go wild.

Imagine what he can do with those fingers!

"You're staring," he said.

She winced. "I'm not." That had to be the biggest lie of the year.

"I know you want me. All you have to say is *'I love you,'* and you'll have me."

She cleared her throat. "Well, I'm—"

"—not ready yet." He finished.

Faye had no answer to that. Desire for him was there, something that hadn't been there before had awakened, but was it more than just lust?

She couldn't tell. Sure, he was doing a good job of trying to make her love him, but was the attraction strong enough?

Would it die once she'd had him a few times?

"Done." Silver closed the bag. "Let's go." He grabbed her hand and tugged toward the door, only to freeze.

Faye gasp, staring at the man who blocked the way out. Soul.

The cyborg soldier.

He pointed the biggest gun she'd ever seen directly *at* them, and there was no more kindness in his eyes.

Soul was dressed in a black armor suit that hugged his muscular body. His bright hair was combed back. He was also in defense-mode.

He'd use the gun, if he had to. Without a doubt.

"Oh, my God," she blurted.

Soul didn't look the slightest pleased. Anger radiated from his beautiful shining eyes. "I was kind of expecting more from you, Faye, but I guess being bound to a former Fighter makes you do things you never thought you'd do."

She blinked. "What?"

"It didn't take much to figure out that someone had messed with Jade's laptop and the codes to this place had been stolen. I suspected it already at Shade and Phoebe's house." He looked at Silver, his gaze deadly. "I guess old habits die hard, right, Silver?"

Silver seemed just as confused as she was, then he smiled. "Well, you know me. Always doing something for an adrenaline kick. Hacking Jade's laptop was a piece of cake. She should upgrade her defense system."

Of course.

Soul believed it'd been Silver who'd hacked Jade's laptop. Good.

That meant Hunter and Avril were safe. It also meant *Jade* believed Silver had done it.

"If you come with me peacefully, this doesn't have to end badly," Soul said.

Neither Faye or Silver moved.

Her cyborg's eyes narrowed. "Why are you here?"

Soul frowned. "To stop you from doing whatever you're doing."

She winced, then gasped. "You don't know why we're here, do you?"

"I don't need to. It's not important. What's important is to stop you."

They exchanged gazes. How brainwashed was Soul? His logic didn't make sense, but he seemed to believe every word he said.

Suspicion filled Faye. "What exactly do you know?"

"I don't want to hurt you. Come with me quietly, and no one needs to end up with broken bones." The cyborg soldier ignored the question.

Faye inhaled and her stubbornness peeked its head.

Soul wasn't going to get the chance to ruin this. Too much was at stake.

"You have to let us go, Soul."

He raised an eyebrow. "Do you take me for a fool? I'm taking you to MedAct where you'll both be prosecuted."

"No, you won't."

"And why's that?"

"Because you're going to let us go. You'll move away from the door, lower your gun, and watch us walk away."

Soul blinked, stared at them. Then, he laughed.

The bitter sound sent cold chills down Faye's spine. She'd liked the gentleness in his eyes when they'd first met, despite the sternness that lay beneath, but this was a side of him she didn't want anything to do with.

The anger was real.

The soldier cyborg's laughter died just as fast as it had begun, and his face melded into intensity. His grip on the gun tightened. "Start walking or I'll put a bullet in Silver's leg."

Faye took a shaky breath and raised her free hand. "Wait, please. Listen to what I have to say."

"And *why* should I do that?" he barked.

She only had a few seconds.

He would fire the gun any moment.

She had to go full-out from the start. "Because I saw your pain."

Soul stilled. His irritation turned to suspicion. "What're you talking about?"

"At Phoebe and Shade's. I saw your pain when you spoke of your bound one."

His expression hardened. "You've no right to speak of her!"

If she'd considered him scary before, it was nothing compared to now. Fury radiated from him. His jaw was tense and his lips thinned.

Talking about his bound one had apparently triggered something dark.

A shot went off, hitting the floor next to Silver.

"Shit!" Faye shouted, and instinctively pulled her cyborg to her, away from the danger, but before she was able to do more, Silver forced her behind him.

"If you fire that gun one more time, I'll kill you," he threatened. "I don't give a shit about what you're going through, but I know you're looking for a way out, and we can offer you one."

Soul's fingers trembled. "There's no way out."

Her body shook. She could die any moment if Soul decided to shoot again, but somehow, she found her strength and courage. She moved next to Silver.

He tried to pull her behind him again, but she didn't let him.

She had to have eye-contact with Soul. "There's a way, and we can create it, but if you stop us now, it *will* be shut down. Not just for you, but for *all* cyborgs."

The big soldier didn't move. The hesitation in his eyes was there, but was he … curious, too?

"What do you know about the bond?" Faye asked.

His eyes narrowed. "It's a curse I can't live without."

She shook her head. "No, you *can* live without it, and we think we know how, but for it to become reality, you need to let us go."

"You need to tell me more if you expect me to believe

you," he hissed between his teeth, gripping the gun harder again.

She exchanged a gaze with Silver, and he nodded.

Faye sighed. "All right, I'll tell you."

This conversation only had one exit.

Either he'd believe them and let them go, or they'd be dead within a few minutes.

"Carolyn Williams didn't create the bond because the cyborgs needed it to live. She created it to control them with love. In truth, the bond is a poison, and it's released into the cyborg's system the moment his bound one dies. Only the cyborgs who survive know the truth—the Fighters, but the world doesn't listen."

Soul gave her a dark grin. "You expect me to believe you?"

"No, I don't, but I can prove it."

His eyes widened, a pinch of interest sparkled in them. "How?"

Faye swallowed and reached inside her shoulder bag, pulling out a small portable hard drive and raised her hand, showing it to Soul. She gave Silver a quick glance to make sure he wasn't against this, but he only watched her.

Celise had given her, with Nightmare's approval, her own copy of Alexander Fleming's algorithm, and the female cyborg program.

Since she was Celise's student, she needed to study both to be able to help, but she'd never believed she'd be showing it to a cyborg soldier.

"Can you access it as it is, or do I have to connect it to the computer over there?"

The big soldier moved closer, his gaze focused on the device. His interest was unmistakable, but so was his suspicion.

Why was she doing this?

Soul wasn't trustworthy. He was the enemy, for heaven's sake. Yet, part of her wanted to trust him, to show him that he wasn't alone, and help was within his grasp.

She was surprised Silver wasn't stopping her. This was, without a doubt, a very bad idea, but maybe he hoped for the same as she did.

Soul stilled and lowered the gun slightly. He tilted his head and his gaze unfocused.

Another chill went through Faye. He was reading the hard drive.

He blinked after a few seconds. "There's a defense system in place. I can't access the information without the code."

"Summer loving five hundred twelve," Faye said.

Soul's gaze shot to hers. "What?"

"The code."

"Seriously?"

She shrugged. "This code will give you access to some of the information. It should be enough for you to know we're not lying."

He snorted. "Whatever." Soul's shining eyes returned to the hard drive. He tilted his head again, refocused. A gentle flash came from them, and Faye knew what that meant.

He'd accessed the information.

Meaning, there was no turning back.

Silence filled the room, but on the inside, she was about to burst. The stress was almost overwhelming, and she couldn't get away from obsessing that she'd just made a huge mistake.

Silver should've stopped her. He should've said something!

She spared him a glance, but he only stood there, studying Soul in silence.

He squeezed her hand without looking at her. "It's the right thing to do."

She swallowed. "You think?"

"His mind is already split. Back at Phoebe and Shade's house, I saw it clearly. He wants freedom but doesn't know how to achieve it. Besides, while Hu—" He cleared his throat. "While *I* hacked into Jade's laptop, I read his file. He has a history of not wanting to follow his bound one's orders."

A grin broke out on Faye's lips. "Oh, really?"

Silver squeezed her hand and smiled back.

Maybe this hadn't been such a bad idea after all.

Soul blinked, his gaze landed on them, and slowly, very slowly, as his face became filled with despair and pain, he lowered his gun to his side. "I'm living a lie."

"Every cyborg is," Silver said. "Let us go, and we'll set you free when the time comes."

The soldier stepped aside. "Go."

Faye frowned.

Just like that?

She'd expected some kind of argument, some kind of denial, but instead, he was letting them go.

They moved toward the door.

She expected Soul to change his mind, grab her, and push her back into the room. Silver would go crazy, and chaos would break out, but nothing happened. Soul didn't even look at them as they passed him.

"Wait," the big cyborg barked.

Faye threw a wary look at him, but he wasn't looking at them. Instead, he kept his head turned away … to hide the tears running down his cheeks?

"Four hundred twelve, one hundred two, seventy-five," he said.

"What?" She frowned.

"My phone number. Memorize it."

"I have it," Silver said. "We'll be in touch."

Soul bit his lip. His agony evident and clear. "I didn't come alone. There are three others. Be careful."

Faye tensed. Damn it, but what had she expected? That MedAct would only send one cyborg soldier to this place?

Ice slid down her spine. Celise, Wind, and the others were out there. What if something happened to them?

The urge to run took over.

Silver was just behind her, with the bag in his hand as they dashed down the long hallways between the high pallet racks.

It was dark, not easy to see, and the scent of metal was all around them. Boxes loaded with God knew what, and machines that meant nothing to Faye.

At least they had what they'd come for. Hopefully, so did the others, but with the cyborg soldiers sneaking around, there was a risk of failure.

Of great failure.

Soul wouldn't get in their way, but she doubted he'd help them. His mind was, without a doubt, in chaos right now.

Boom!

Faye froze. Her heart stuttered. It'd been the most frightening sound she'd ever heard, echoing in her ears.

Silver almost ran her over when she stopped. His fear just as evident as hers.

A cyborg screamed, and the voice sounded way too familiar.

Nightmare.

"No," she gasped, and they took off again.

CHAPTER 24

The closer they got to where Celise, Nightmare, and the others were, the more sounds she endured. One cyborg shouted something, another screamed, as if in pain. There was running and grunting, and another gun went off.

Despair filled Faye, and all she could do was imagining her friends going down each time a shot was heard. Hopefully, she was wrong.

They were heading in the direction of danger, but there was no other way for them to go. She wouldn't abandon them, and neither would Silver.

"Stay close to me," he said, his gaze serious. "I'll protect you."

"Don't play a hero. I won't forgive you if you sacrifice yourself for me."

He grinned. "See. You do care about me."

Usually, she'd snort something back, but this time, the

denial and protests didn't come. "Yeah, I do."

Their gazes met, and Silver's grin faded.

Maybe he saw what she felt on the inside. He meant more to her than she'd ever imagined he would. The realization slowly swept over her. Lately, she'd enjoyed every minute she'd spent with him, but it wasn't until now that she understood what was happening to her, now when both of them risked death.

The thought of losing him was unbearable.

Funny how things could change in a matter of days.

They turned a corner and Faye spotted the warehouse exit. Even if it was dark outside, the exit was lit up from all kinds of flashlights. Something told her those beams of light came from the guns that belonged to the cyborg soldiers.

A cyborg lay on the ground just outside the exit, and two people leaned over him. It took only a few more steps for Faye to recognize the cyborg as Nightmare. Wind and Celise were next to him.

Blood.

So much blood.

The ground beneath the leader was dark red, and his hair was a thick and wet mess. He wasn't moving, and his eyes were closed. Was he breathing?

Was he alive?

Her heart clenched. It was like running straight into a fight scene from some gruesome movie. "Oh, my God." It was almost impossible to hold back the tears, and just as shocking to cry over Nightmare. Perhaps she cared about him, too.

He was the leader of the Fighters, after all. He was important.

Without him, the Fighters would fall apart.

He was the one holding them together.

Celise raised her head when she heard them. Her eyes were filled with fear and tears. Her hands trembled as she pressed them against Nightmare's forehead. They were covered in blood, too. Dark red stains were all over her clothes, and even her cheeks and hair.

Wind's grim expression was one Faye had never seen before. This usually calm and gentle cyborg was boiling with anger, but when he spotted them, the fury eased. "Did you get the stuff?"

"Yes," Faye slid to her knees. "We got everything. What happened?"

They were surrounded by chaos. Heaven roared as he punched a cyborg soldier in the face, but the soldier barely budged. Instead, he hit Heaven back, punching the Fighter to the ground.

Other Fighters joined in, jumping the three cyborg soldiers encircling him, delivering punches and kicks, but the soldiers were stronger.

A lot stronger.

At least Soul wasn't in the picture. She had no idea if he'd join the fight or not, but she hoped he'd stay away.

Cyborg soldiers had been created to be superior to the regular cyborgs. They were the perfect killing machines, and they were the only ones who could take out a cyborg, and they seemed to be doing a good job.

One Fighter was already on the ground. If Heaven was alive, Faye couldn't tell, but her heart broke even more, and the desperation exploded in her chest.

This was not supposed to happen!

"One of the bastards shot him. He didn't stand a chance," Celise gritted her teeth and sniffed as she looked at the rogue leader. "He's alive, but I don't know for how long. The bullet is still in his head."

Faye barely dared to imagine the damage the bullet had done. Even if Nightmare was alive, would he still be the same? Would he ever wake up?

A human's chances of surviving a bullet to the head were limited. What if it was the same for a cyborg?

Faye noticed the second van was gone. "Where's the big van?"

"The cyborg soldiers showed up just after we loaded the tank into the van. Sense and Phoenix managed to get away with it. No one followed them."

A small part of her relaxed. At least her two friends were safe.

Heaven groaned and moved where he was lying.

Thank God he was alive! But for how much longer?

He jumped to his feet and joined the fight again. "Go!" he roared. "We can't hold them much longer!"

The soldiers' legs trembled and with each punch the Fighters delivered, they became slower. Getting hit back didn't improve the situation. Somehow, they'd managed to

211

take down one cyborg soldier, but that was far from enough. It was just a matter of time before the Fighters would be taken care of, and once that happened, the cyborg soldiers would come for *them*.

For her, Celise, Wind, Silver, and Nightmare.

Her adrenaline spiked.

They needed to act.

Now.

"We have to move him," she said. "We have no other choice."

Even if she'd been mentally prepared for this situation, it still felt surreal, but even if her mind had a hard time processing everything, Faye's body didn't.

Without a second thought, she stepped aside so Silver could approach Nightmare.

At least no one was shooting at them anymore. Instead, the cyborg soldiers seemed focused on muscle-strength.

The sounds of pain and the loud groans echoed in her head, increasing her stress and tension.

Faye took the bag with medicine from Silver.

He and Wind lifted the unconscious Nightmare. The big dark cyborg hung between them, but they were strong enough to carry him.

The wound on Nightmare's forehead looked nasty. It didn't stop bleeding, and his skin was pale. Too pale for Faye's liking.

"Stay behind us," Wind instructed her and Celise. "I'll drive."

"What about Heaven and the others?" the doctor asked as they hurried toward the van. Her voice trembled.

"Save him!" Heaven roared as if he'd heard her.

Faye shot him a glance and the other four Fighters who were doing everything in their power to keep the cyborg soldiers away from her and the others.

They were beaten badly, only seemed to be standing thanks to their rage and pure stubbornness.

Guilt filled her. She should've at least asked the four Fighters their names. Now, they were doomed. Heaven, too.

She didn't want to leave them behind. Neither did Celise, Wind, or Silver. She saw it written all over their faces, but there was no other choice.

Their sacrifice wouldn't be in vain. They'd figure out how to remove the bond and release all cyborgs. Hopefully, Heaven and the four Fighters would still be alive when that day came.

They reached the van, and Celise threw the doors open. She and Faye jumped in and reached for Nightmare as Silver and Wind laid him on the van's floor.

Wind ran for the front as she and the doctor pulled Nightmare in.

The leader didn't make a sound; didn't even stir.

He was terribly quiet. Too quiet.

Celise was instantly on him, taking out a medkit and started putting pressure against the wound.

As Wind jumped behind the wheel, Silver jumped in in the back and reached for the doors.

"No!" someone yelled.

Faye raised her head to see where the shout had come from. Her gaze found Heaven.

His eyes and face showed no emotions, but his body did.

A cyborg soldier wrapped his arms around Heaven's waist as the Fighter reached for another soldier.

It was like watching a robot, because of Heaven's motionless face, but when she looked at the cyborg soldier, everything in Faye stopped.

It was as if time itself halted when the cyborg soldier lifted his big gun and point it in their direction.

A gasp left her mouth and—

Boom!

She flinched, almost jumped out of her own skin when Silver closed the doors and the van took off.

Thank God.

The shot missed.

The sound had been deafening, but they were safe now.

The cyborg soldiers wouldn't come after them.

Heaven and the others would make sure of that. They'd give them enough time to get away, and by then, it would be pointless for the soldiers to even try to catch them.

"How's he doing?" she asked Celise.

Nightmare looked worse by the minute, but the doctor had managed to stop the bleeding.

"I don't know, but it doesn't look promising."

Faye had only seen her friend this worried one time before—when Wind had been dying.

214

"We *must* save him," Celise said with tear-filled eyes.

She reached for her phone. "I'm calling Blaze." She pushed his number, and a few rings later, Blaze picked up.

"Yes?"

"Get ready. Nightmare's wounded."

A gasp came from the other side of the line. "Where?"

"He's been shot in the head."

A long chant of curse words left Blaze's mouth. "We'll be ready." He hung up.

Faye put away the phone. "Can I help?"

"Have an eye on his pulse. We have a long ride back."

She nodded and placed two fingers to his throat. "Step on it, Wind!" She didn't get an answer back, but the van accelerated, almost making her lose her balance.

Silver groaned.

Her cyborg had been quiet since the doors had been shut, just sitting in the same position.

Guilt filled her. He needed her too, but Nightmare was hurt.

Silver groaned again.

Worry filled her. "Silver?"

Slowly, he turned and met her gaze. His face was twisted in agony and fear, his hands trembled—and they were red from blood.

Blood that also stained his chest.

The bullet hadn't missed.

It'd hit him in the chest.

Silver collapsed on the floor.

"Silver!"

CHAPTER 25

The hour it took to get back to the Fighters' headquarters was the longest in Faye's life. Her body trembled, stress overwhelmed her, and her heart ached, as she sat on the van floor with a bleeding Silver in her arms.

Tears pushed behind her eyes, but she managed to stay strong and hold them back. The last thing he needed right now was to see her cry.

She and Celise had done everything in their power to keep Nightmare and Silver alive. Both cyborgs had lost too much blood. Both were pale, but thankfully, they'd managed to stop the bleeding. Now, only time could tell how this would end.

Silver gave Faye a lazy look, sleep slowly taking him.

She shook him. "Don't you dare die on me. Keep your eyes open."

He smiled but didn't say anything. Instead, he squeezed

her hand and leaned his head against her palm.

The only hope she had was that cyborgs were stronger than humans, and they healed faster. Even if Silver had been hit in the chest, he was still alive. A human would've been dead by now.

The bullet seemed to have missed his lungs since he was breathing normally, but who knew what other damage had been done. Judging by the way he looked, she was minutes away from losing him.

"Damn it, Wind! How much further?"

"Almost there."

The van turned and the sound of gravel under tires hit her ears. They *were* close.

Blaze and a few other Fighters were waiting for them, ready to help Silver and Nightmare. She'd made a second call to Blaze, telling him about her cyborg.

He'd cursed even louder than the first time when she'd told him the bad news about their leader.

Not only were Nightmare and Silver hurt, they'd lost five Fighters, and no one knew if they'd ever see them again.

Faye doubted MedAct would give Heaven and the others the chance to bind themselves. MedAct would do something else to them. What, she barely dared to imagine.

The van came to a halt, and seconds later, the doors flung open.

A worried Blaze stood there with two other Fighters. They took a fast assessment of the situation, then got to work.

Nightmare and Silver were lifted from the van and carried toward the elevator that would take them underground and to the Fighters' headquarters.

Faye ached every time Silver groaned or made a face from pain. His body trembled, but at least, he was alive … for now.

Nightmare, on the other hand, was silent. Not even a twitch of an eye.

A Fighter took the van, while she and the others went down.

"Everything's ready for them," Blaze said, studying his patients. His fear was unmistakable.

She didn't even want to think about what would happen if Nightmare died. She didn't want to think about what would happen to *her* if Silver died. She'd never ached this badly for anyone. Despite his annoying personality, she'd grown fond of him to a level she'd never seen coming.

He was in her heart now.

He'd taken over her soul.

And he was dying.

"I want to help," Faye told Blaze.

He nodded. "We're going to need every hand we can get."

"I'll take care of Nightmare," Celise said and looked at Blaze, "while you help Silver."

"Agreed."

Faye went forward, as if in a trance. The world around her blurred. She barely noticed all the Fighters that watched them with an agonizing silence as they passed by the gathering room.

Blood dripped onto the floor from both Silver and Nightmare, but no one moved to clean it up.

A Fighter ran ahead and threw open the doors to the infirmary. Seconds later, the room was filled with activity. Fighters were there, dressed, cleaned, and ready to take care of their leader and Silver.

"Go and clean up while we begin," Blaze told her.

Faye instantly ran to the cleaning room that was located next to the infirmary. Celise and Wind were just behind her.

Being ordered around was one of the things she hated most, but right now, she'd do whatever he asked of her. She sterilized her hands the way Celise had shown her, scrubbing them hard and as fast as she could possibly manage. Barely a minute later, Faye threw on the hair net, the surgical scrubs, and the mask before returning to the infirmary with the others.

She watched Blaze sedate Silver, and when he closed his eyes frigid tremor traveled down her spine. What if that had been the last time she'd ever seen his beautiful shining eyes?

"We need to get the bullet out," Blaze said as other Fighters gathered around the gurney Silver lay on.

The same thing was happening around the gurney Nightmare was on. Celise was already working, a deep frown on her forehead. Wind was by her side.

Faye's focus returned to Silver. A cringe went through her as Blaze cut him open, nausea hitting her hard, but she remained on her legs.

She couldn't let him die.

CHAPTER 26

"Don't you dare die on me, you hear me?"

That voice.

It sounded familiar.

"I need you, more than ever. I understand that now. Please, don't leave me."

Faye.

She was so near. He felt her breath against his ear, as she whispered her words, and yet, she was so far away.

Silver was unable to reach her, unable to let her know he heard her. The darkness he swam in had a tight grip on him.

"Your mission has succeeded, do you know that? I've given in as well. Now, come back to me."

His heart made a flip.

Did it mean she ... loved him?

"I think I've felt like this for a while, but it wasn't until you got hurt that I understood my feelings. The thought of losing you

hurt like nothing I've ever experienced. It was my stubbornness that kept me from seeing the truth."

Something touched his arm, something tiny and gentle. Her hand?

"I'll tell you all about it. Just come back to me."

Her voice faded, and for a long time, all he knew was silence and darkness.

Silver opened his dry and tired eyes. He stared at the familiar ceiling and inhaled the just as familiar scents from the infirmary in the Fighters' headquarters.

He was home.

How had he gotten here?

The last thing he remembered was lying on Faye's knees in the van as they rushed back.

Everything hurt. His muscles ached, but at least he was alive. The bed he lay on was comfortable and soft. He even felt fresh, as if he'd been cleaned.

Silver blinked and turned his head, meeting the gaze of a smiling Blaze, but the smile didn't reach the Fighter's sad eyes. He searched for Faye, but she wasn't there.

Blaze was the only one in the room.

Someone lay on the bed next to him.

"Welcome back," the medic cyborg said and approached. "How're you feeling?"

A groan left his lips when he tried to speak. "Bruised, but fine. Where's Faye? Is she all right?"

He nodded. "She's fine, but worries about you. She's been glued to your side since you got back, so I sent her away a few hours ago to get some rest. She looked drained."

Silver frowned, but his heart sang from joy. Maybe all the things he'd heard while he was out had been real. "She was by my side?"

"Yes. She refused to leave you. She even helped me piece you together."

He placed his hand on his bandaged chest, remembering when he'd been shot. Agony still echoed in his mind, along with the terrified look in Faye's eyes when she realized what'd happened.

"You've been kept in a coma for three days, so we could heal you," Blaze said. "Thanks to some of the medicine you and Faye got, we were able to speed up the process, by programming your cells to work ten times faster. It would've been a painful experience if you'd been awake."

Silver nodded, not really caring about the healing. All he had in his mind was Faye.

He needed to go to her.

He grunted as he tried to sit. His body was stiff. Obviously, he had some healing left to do, but this, he could live with. A little bit of pain wouldn't stop him from going to Faye.

His gaze locked on the bed next to him and he froze.

Nightmare.

His leader lay still, slowly breathing, connected to machines that made beeping sounds.

A cold chill went through him and the memories flushed through him.

Nightmare had been shot in the head, but they'd managed to get him into the van before he himself had been shot.

Heaven and four other Fighters had been left behind.

Silver clenched his fists and pressed his lips together. "What's wrong with him?"

The sadness in Blaze's eyes intensified.

Now he understood why.

"We're keeping him in a coma. He's healing well, but we have no idea how this is going to end."

His chest tightened. He didn't want to think about what would happen if Nightmare died. "What about Heaven and the others?"

Blaze remained silent for a moment. "I've no idea. We tried to track them with Celise's program, but they're gone. No trace whatsoever. They haven't been brought to MedAct."

Silver tried to calm his nerves. "We have to find them."

"We're doing everything we can."

That meant Heaven and the others were lost, and the chances of finding them were slim.

He stood. "Thank you for saving me."

The medic gave him a nod. "Of course."

"I need to go to Faye."

The way to her former room was longer than he remembered. Silver wanted to run, but his muscles objected. It would take a few more days before he was himself again, but the ache wouldn't stop him from holding and kissing her.

All the things he'd heard. They'd been real, right?

A string of hope carried him further, moving closer to his beloved bound one with each step he took.

The memory of Claire swept through his mind, making him slow.

Claire.

She, with the beautiful smile and always a kind word to everyone. She, who'd loved life, and hadn't deserved the ending she'd gotten, but the funny thing was, he'd barely thought of her since Faye had come into his life.

Only one year ago, he'd been oblivious to all this. He'd still been with Claire, but now, his life was so different.

The ache in his chest, the need for a bound one wasn't there anymore. Instead, it'd been replaced with love and desire.

The bond wasn't demanding a bound one anymore.

It demanded nearness, sweet words, and wild nights between the sheets.

He smiled. His life *had* changed. At first, Silver had cursed his fate, but now, he embraced it.

If Faye had done the same, they could be happy together.

He was tired of all the pain, all the misery. He wanted to be happy again, and he'd do everything in his power to get that.

His hope intensified.

Silver stopped in front Faye's room and put his hand on the handle. He closed his eyes. "Please, let everything I heard be true."

Slowly, he pushed the handle down and entered the room with silent steps.

She lay on the bed, asleep, with streaks from tears on her cheeks. She was hugging the pillow and her knees were pulled up to her stomach.

Air got stuck in his throat.

She'd been crying.

For him?

His hands trembled as he reached for her. The need to be near Faye intensified to overwhelming levels, making it difficult to breathe.

He'd be her protector, he'd be her lover and friend. He'd be anything she wanted him to be.

As long as she was alive, he'd be there.

He'd be the cyborg a bound one deserved.

Silver wasn't against the bond anymore. He'd embraced it completely. Even more than before, when he'd told her.

He was truly bound to Faye now.

There was no other way to go, and he didn't mind. Despite the bad things with the bond, it did bring him happiness once he chose to accept it.

Silver knelt in front of the bed and leaned over her, studying her sleeping face, drowning in her beauty. He could stay like this forever, just admiring what was his.

On paper, he was the one who belonged to her, but he didn't give a damn about it. In his eyes, she was just as much his as he was hers.

An image of Claire appeared in his mind again, and he

tensed. Why was he thinking of Claire all of a sudden?

He'd missed her painfully every day since her sudden death, but once Faye had initiated a new bond, his focus had been on her. Claire had been pushed back somewhere into his subconsciousness.

He sighed.

The bond was a fickle thing, but Claire no longer mattered. What mattered was here and now. Claire was long gone, and Faye was here.

His bound one was here.

That was all he needed.

With a gentle smile, Silver leaned down and placed a slow kiss on her cheek. Feeling her warm soft skin against his lips made his heart jump. The bond demanded more.

He *had* to wrap his arms around her and love her all night long but resisted the urge. Silver needed to know what he'd heard had been real first.

His idea of not having sex with her as long as she didn't love him had come back to bite him many times, but somehow, he'd managed to stay strong. If he'd given in it would've left an empty feeling in his chest.

Faye stirred, and he sat on the bed, waiting for her to fully wake up.

She yawned, and smacked her lips, as if her mouth was dry.

Silver chuckled, not expecting to find such a thing cute, but he did. "At least, you don't snore."

Her eyes shot open and she gasped when she locked eyes

with him. "Oh, my God! You're awake." She sat up so fast and wrapped her arms around him, he barely had a chance to react.

He groaned when discomfort surged through his body, but his smile didn't fade. Instead, her eagerness spiked his excitement.

Maybe, her words had been real after all.

"Easy. I'm still achy all over."

She instantly pulled back. "So sorry. I didn't mean to hurt you."

"I know." Silver put his hand against her cheek, looking deep into her eyes, drying away the traces of her tears. "You don't have to cry anymore. I'm fine and alive."

Faye flashed a wide smile, but more tears ran down her cheeks.

He chuckled and shook his head. "I guess you'll never listen to me."

"I thought I was going to lose you."

He leaned closer. "Oh, really? So, you're admitting you missed me, you can't live without me."

She frowned. "I see your personality is back at its peak."

Silver hovered over her, sealing her in between his arms as she lay down. "Of course. Did you expect me to change just because I've been shot in the chest?" He expected a cocky remark back, but she remained silent instead, just meeting his gaze, as if admiring the view.

Then she reached for his face. "No. I love you just the way you are."

He froze. His heart pounded so hard it almost hurt. "What?"

"Did you lose your hearing somewhere along the way? I said I love you just the way you are." Faye grinned.

He was unable to come up with anything cocky to say. "So, everything I heard while I was sleeping *was* real. I thought I'd dreamt it."

Her eyes widened. "You heard me?"

Silver nodded. "You said my mission had been successful; you'd given in, you understand your feelings. I wanted to find out if those words had been a dream or not from the moment I woke up."

She blushed, and a gentle smile played on her lips. "You didn't imagine anything."

Silver blinked. He'd half-expected her words to be his imagination, and that he'd find a Faye who still didn't want anything to do with him.

Instead, she looked at him as if he was her greatest treasure.

It was a look that pulled him in and he was unable to stop himself.

He pressed a gentle kiss to her lips. Somehow, he still half-expected to be pushed away. Maybe in the back of his mind, he waited to see the old Faye, but when she wrapped her arms around him with sweet caresses, his entire body ignited.

Goosebumps awakened on his skin, and he inhaled deeply as a bolt of desire shot through him. The desire sparked into a fire when she unbuttoned his shirt.

Their gazes met.

"Don't expect me to wait anymore," Faye said as her hands explored his chest. "I'll only stop if you're in too much pain."

Silver grinned and threw his shirt to the floor. "A few bruises won't stop me."

"Good. Start stripping."

He chuckled but did as she wanted. He stood, and without breaking eye contact, he removed his pants and underwear.

Her big eyes that were filled with curiosity and anticipation drove him.

She wanted him.

She actually wanted him.

About time.

Silver was just about to climb under the covers when Faye sat on the edge of the bed. He stilled but didn't miss how her passionate gaze lingered on his body, taking in every inch of him, eating him up with the passion in her eyes.

His breath got stuck in his throat.

Claire had never looked at him the way Faye did now. He'd never seen *this* kind of hunger in his former bound one's eyes. It was something new, and it made blood rush to his shaft.

There was no doubt or shyness in Faye's gaze. She knew what she wanted and what she needed.

His grin widened. Even if he hadn't believed it at first, he believed it now.

Faye was the right one for him.

They would, without a doubt, argue and disagree all the time, but they'd just as passionately love and cherish each other.

She crooked a finger at him. "Come closer, big boy."

Silver had no plans to disobey, and when her small fingers wrapped around his erection with a firm grip, he couldn't stop his hiss.

The sound seemed to please her, and as she wrapped her lips around him, she let out a satisfied moan of her own.

His entire body jerked from the sudden and intense feeling that shot through him. He trembled, and his knees weakened. It'd been such a long time since he'd felt something that incredible.

He couldn't recall it being this amazing. The way she swirled her tongue around his tip, and the way her hands caressed and teased him sent his whole world into a spin.

Faye took her time, licking and sucking him until he barely could take it anymore. Only then did she let him go and stood. She dried her mouth with a grin. "I'm far from done with you. Lay down."

Silver was on the bed within a second and watched her throw off her clothes.

She was apparently in a hurry, but when he reached for her, she slapped his hand. He frowned.

Her wicked grin widened as she straddled him. "You can

touch me all you want later. Tonight's my turn."

Silver was about to object, but when she went for his throat and showered him with sweet kisses, all he could do was groan. He'd thought about their first *real* time many times.

He'd imagined candle lights, calm music, and making love for hours. Never had he imagined Faye would be the one in control, and it would be fast and hard, but that was exactly where this was heading.

She was all over him, sweeping him further and further away, making him lose his mind, and making the bond sing in his chest.

He enjoyed and thrived in every kiss, caress, and nip.

She was gentle. Silver doubted she didn't see all his bruises, but she was also in a hurry, and he didn't care anymore that his fantasies of how he'd wanted this to go down were shattered.

He enjoyed *this* a thousand times more.

Faye grabbed his arousal and placed herself over it.

He tensed, anticipation singing within him as he waited for that amazing feeling.

When she finally sank down on him, surrounding him with the sensation of her warm flesh, he couldn't hold back his gasp, and he arched his back.

Faye was more than ready for him. She didn't even give herself time to adapt to his size, maybe she didn't need to.

Instead, she took him on a wild ride, and all he could do was tag along, surrendering to her demanding desire.

Silver closed his eyes and wrapped his arms around her.

Enjoying every sensation her body took him through. The sounds from their lovemaking filled the room.

Every groan, every gasp, and moan spiked his desire further. The crash from the bed's headboard banging against the wall faded into the distance when she kissed him.

If she continued like this, Silver wouldn't be able to hold on much longer. Her relentless ride took him to levels he couldn't recall ever experiencing.

He'd been living with his broken bond ever since Claire died, and that'd filled him with a frustration so deep it'd been difficult to think sometimes, and the desire for a new bound one had almost driven him crazy. Now, when she rode him as if there was no tomorrow, he wouldn't last.

Faye tensed around him, squeezing him like a glove, and shouting out her orgasm.

That was it.

With no possibility of stopping it, he felt himself coming. His body went taut, like a board beneath her and shook violently as he filled her. It seemed to go on forever, blowing his mind from the intensity, and once he'd finally collapsed from exhaustion, Silver could barely lift a muscle.

She collapsed on top of him, panting.

He stared at the ceiling, breathing just as heavily as she, but he'd never felt this satisfied in his entire life. "You sure know how to make a cyborg happy."

Faye raised her head and grinned. Her cheeks were flushed, but a deep satisfaction lingered in her gaze. "I sure do." She lay down by his side.

Silver wrapped his arms around her as she placed her

head on his chest. "There definitely is nothing wrong with your self-esteem."

"Of course not, and don't ever expect it to be."

He could only smile. "I don't." He took a deep breath. "I guess this means you're keeping me."

She raised her head and frowned. "Were you expecting me to run away?"

Silver remained silent for a moment. "For a long time, you didn't show any interest, not even after I gave in to the bond. I wasn't sure what to think."

"And yet, you never gave up on making me fall in love with you." Faye touched his chest, avoiding the place where he'd been shot. "Honestly, I think I fell in love with you early on, I just refused to see it or accept it since you hated what I'd done to you."

He caressed her arm lazily. "I did, but not anymore. Giving in to the bond was the best thing I've ever done."

A smile spread on her lips. "Really?"

"Really." He rolled to his side and captured her gaze. "I love you. Even if those feelings were forced upon me because of the bond, they're here to stay. Even if accepting them took some time, I'm fine with it now, and I intend to live my life like the cyborg you deserve, but just don't expect my personality to change. I'll still drive you crazy every other day."

Faye laughed. "You're a bastard."

He grinned and caressed her cheek. "I know, but that's why you love me."

EPILOGUE

Beep…

The machine that Nightmare was attached to let out a low sound. Celise raised her eyes, read the numbers on the display, and wrote them down in her notebook.

Nothing had changed.

Everything was still the same, but at the same time, everything was different. It'd been several days since they'd returned with all the equipment.

They had everything they needed to create the first female cyborg, but the rogue leader was still not waking up.

Something was wrong.

It was unusual, seeing this big dark cyborg being so immobile. His usually aggressive and defensive expression wasn't there anymore. Instead, his face was calm, revealing his beauty in a way she hadn't seen before.

She couldn't help but feel sorry for him. He'd been

through so much. No wonder he'd developed thick skin. There weren't many people he trusted, but she'd managed to become one of the few.

Celise shook her head and snorted. The last thing she'd ever imagined was finding herself there, in the Fighters' headquarters, taking care of their leader.

Everything told her he was dangerous, deadly, and unpredictable.

The media did a good job depicting him as a monster, but in a way, he was one.

He'd been forced into a role he didn't want. Celise didn't doubt that.

There was no love in Nightmare's heart. No emotions, just determination, and pure stubbornness. That was what had kept him alive ... until now.

Blaze entered the infirmary. His red hair was in a ponytail and his shining eyes had a serious glint as he approached the bed. "Any change?"

She shook her head. "No. He's stable, but I can't figure out what's wrong with him. The medicine we brought back has healed him, just as it healed Silver, but why isn't he waking up?"

The medic cyborg studied his leader. "All the scans show his body is fine. He *should* be awake by now. We've taken him out of the coma." He went silent for a while. "What if the damage isn't physical?"

Celise tensed. "Do you think it's in his programming?"

"It might be. We should take a look."

She grabbed the machine that stood in the corner of the room and placed it on the small table next to the bed. It was about the size of a laptop, but as thick as three books. Frustration filled her. "Why didn't we think of this sooner?"

"Don't blame yourself. We're all tired."

She sighed. "True." Celise unbuttoned Nightmare's shirt, revealing his fit chest, but only paid attention to what she was doing. She reached for the cords to the machine and attached them to the leader's chest and forehead.

The machine beeped, and the digital screen came on.

Celise pushed a long sequence of numbers.

The machine got to work, looking deep into Nightmare's program, scanning every little part of it.

Minutes passed in silence, then, finally, the device let out a loud sound before going silent.

She looked at the screen with a thundering heart. She gasped.

Blaze came around the bed with worry in his expression and scanned the screen. "Oh, my God. It's worse than I thought. His basic program has been damaged. Healing him won't fix this, and as it is right now, he'll never wake up." He looked at Celise. "Can you fix him?"

She dried away the stubborn tear that ran down her cheek. "This is beyond my level of expertise. I'm years away from learning how to create cyborgs. The female cyborg program is complete, but how to write or repair a program … I've no idea how to do that."

Silence filled the large room.

The machine attached to Nightmare beeped.

"So, what do we do?" the medic asked with a shaky voice.

The machine beeped again …

… and again.

Celise stared at Nightmare.

Beep …

Beep …

She pinned Blaze with a look, determination washed over her. "We need Jade."

THANK YOU

Thank you for reading my story. I hope you enjoyed it.
If you're interested in more, you can now read book four in
the Bound by Her series - *Fierce Cyborg*.
Nightmare's and Jade's story.

PREVIOUS BOOKS IN THE SERIES:

Her Cyborg - Book 1
Tempted Cyborg - Book 1.5
Loved Cyborg - Book 2

ABOUT THE AUTHOR

Nellie C. Lind lives in Sweden with her son, but she was born in Poland. Writing has always been one of her greatest interests. Today, she runs the publishing house, Sense of Romance.

She writes passionate paranormal romance, fantasy, and science fiction books for adult readers. You'll find all sorts of beings in her stories, such as angels, vampires, gods, and elves.

You'll also find everything from short stories to novels among her books. Keep an eye open for upcoming releases!

Website: nellieclind.com
Blog: sense-of-romance.com